Cat O
Of Hell

Ple

Truss is an award-winning columnist, broadcaster
comedy radio dramatist, and the author of the
menally successful *Eats, Shoots & Leaves*. She recently
the unheard-of switch of allegiance from cats to
This novel — her first for more than ten years — is
perhaps inevitable result.

Praise for *Cat Out Of Hell*

'*Cat Out Of Hell* isn't unlike Sherlock Holmes solving
The Master and Margarita with the help of Jeeves'
The Times

'A wonderful tale full of parodies, pastiches and
paradoxes . . . pure joy'
Daily Telegraph

'Full of trademark dry Truss humour and lovely
rary references . . . You may never look at a cat in
the same way again'
Daily Mail

12622974

'One of those rare books that actually makes you laugh out loud . . . impossible not to read in one sitting'
Sunday Times

'A novel as entertaining as it is addictive . . . the best in humorous writing'
Sunday Telegraph

'Truss brings an eerie, 19th-century kind of horror into the present-day world'
Guardian

'A comic chiller in the best tradition of mad British humour'
Daily Express

'Warm humour was what made *Eats, Shoots & Leaves* a hit and she hasn't lost her touch'
Evening Standard

'Very funny indeed'
Sunday Express

'Genuinely creepy at times . . . also hilarious. Just be prepared to view cats with a certain amount of suspicion from now on'
Press Association

'The greatest feline I've encountered since Saki's Tobermory . . . hilarious and genuinely shivery. A gorgeous piece of escapism'
Saga Magazine

'A Gothic tale guaranteed to surprise, move and entertain'
Woman's Weekly

'An inventive tale that's sure to make you smile. Even if you're a dog person'
SFX

'Tremendous fun'
SciFi Now

Also by Lynne Truss

Fiction
With One Lousy Free Packet of Seed
Tennyson's Gift
Going Loco
A Certain Age

Non Fiction
Making the Cat Laugh
Eats, Shoots & Leaves: The Zero Tolerance Approach
to Punctuation
Talk to the Hand: The Utter Bloody Rudeness of Everyday Life
Get Her Off the Pitch!: How Sport Took Over My Life
Tennyson and his Circle

For Children
Eats, Shoots & Leaves: Why, Commas Really Do Make
a Difference!
The Girl's Like Spaghetti: Why, You Can't Manage
Without Apostrophes!
Twenty-Odd Ducks: Why, Every Punctuation Mark Counts!

Lynne Truss

Cat Out Of Hell

Published by Arrow Books in association with Hammer 2014

1 3 5 7 9 10 8 6 4 2

Copyright © Lynne Truss 2014

Lynne Truss has asserted her right under the Copyright, Designs
and Patents Act, 1988, to be identified as the author of this work

This is a work of fiction. Names and characters are the product of the author's
imagination and any resemblance to actual persons, living or dead, is entirely
coincidental.

This book is sold subject to the condition that it shall not, by way of trade or
otherwise, be lent, resold, hired out, or otherwise circulated without the publisher's
prior consent in any form of binding or cover other than that in which it is published
and without a similar condition, including this condition, being imposed on the
subsequent purchaser.

First published in Great Britain in 2014 by
Arrow Books in association with Hammer
Random House, 20 Vauxhall Bridge Road,
London SW1V 2SA

A Penguin Random House Company

Penguin
Random House
UK

www.randomhouse.co.uk

Addresses for companies within The Random House Group Limited can be found at:
www.randomhouse.co.uk/offices.htm

The Random House Group Limited Reg. No. 954009

A CIP catalogue record for this book
is available from the British Library

ISBN 9780099585343

MIX
Paper from
responsible sources
FSC® C018179

Penguin Random House is committed to a sustainable
future for our business, our readers and our planet.
This book is made from Forest Stewardship
Council® certified paper.

Typeset by Palimpsest Book Production Ltd, Falkirk, Stirlingshire
Printed and bound by CPI Group (UK) Ltd, Croydon, CR0 4YY

To Gemma,
who loves proper horror,
with apologies

PART ONE

Beside the Sea

The following story, which is absolutely true, was brought to my attention when I was holidaying recently on the coast of North Norfolk. The month was January. I was in search of silence and tranquillity. I had rented a cottage which provided a fine view of the deserted nearby seashore, on which my small brown dog could run in safety. Having recently suffered the loss of my dear wife, I chose the location with care — isolation was precisely what I required, for I was liable to sudden bouts of uncontrollable emotion, and wished not to be the cause of distress or discomfort in others. For a week or two, I was glad to be alone there: to make the fire, cook simple meals, watch the dog running in happy circles at the far-off water's edge, and weep freely in private whenever the need overcame me.

But I forgot that I would need mental stimulus. At the end of Michaelmas term I had bid farewell to my position at the library in Cambridge with few real regrets; the work had been mechanical for quite some time, and I had assumed I would not miss it. I remember debating whether to pack my laptop. This is strange to think of now. Had I not brought it with me, perhaps the following story would never have been told. But pack it I did. And one stormy evening, when the wind was moaning in the chimney and I was craving intellectual occupation, I remembered that, around the close of the year, a library member of small acquaintance had sent to me by email the following folder of documents and other files, under the general title 'Roger'. I opened it gratefully, and for several hours afterwards I was transported by its contents. By turns I was confused, suspicious, impatient and even cynical. The story therein conveyed was outlandish, not to say preposterous. And yet, as I continued to study the material over the ensuing days, I felt increasingly inclined to believe it. Sad to say, I think what finally convinced me of the files' veracity was the staggering stupidity of the man named throughout as 'Wiggy', through whose pitifully inadequate understanding these events are mainly delivered to us. As my wife would have said (I can hear her now), you couldn't make him up.

Naturally, I wondered on occasion what lay behind Dr Winterton's decision to send this material to me. But being unable to make contact with him (no wi-fi here), I was bound to accept the most likely explanation. I had rented a lonely cottage at the seaside; Winterton had somehow heard tell of it; he knew that this story unfolded in a similarly lonely cottage beside the sea. Though I often tried to picture Dr Winterton, I found that I could capture only, in my mind's eye, a fleeting impression of a snaggle tooth and a hollow, unshaven cheek, and possibly (oddly) the smell of cloves. In former times, I would have asked Mary, of course. She had been my colleague at the library for the past twenty years; even though her position was part-time, she had paid lively attention to the members in a way that I would sometimes find bewildering. I remember how she would, on occasion, attempt to discuss the members with me at dinner, and grow incredulous (but amused) when I was able to call to mind not one of the persons concerned. I believe she did once mention Winterton to me in particular, but she would be unsurprised to learn that I could now recollect nothing of the circumstances of her dealings with him. For several years she was in charge of allocating the carrels in the great reading room, so perhaps it was related to that. She was the most wonderful, practical and rational woman, my dear Mary. She would never have taken this simple cottage! She would have been instantly alive to all its frustrating inconveniences. But she would have laughed with sheer pleasure to see our dog running so happily on the deserted shore. Every time he does it, I feel her loss most dreadfully.

After long consideration, I have decided to present this material exactly in the order I encountered it myself. Who is Roger? Wait and see. I hope this is not confusing, but at the same time I have come to believe that I should editorialise as little as possible. I will merely make clear, to begin with, that the 'written' files – including the rather pointless and silly dramatic efforts – are by the man calling himself Wiggy. Descriptions of photographs and transcripts of the audio files are by me.

CONTENTS OF ROGER FOLDER
WORD FILES:
ROGER NOTES (119KB)
ROGER THOUGHTS (66KB)
MORE STUFF (33KB)
ROGER DREAM (40KB)

JPEGS:
DSC00546 (2MB)
DSC00021 (1.6MB)
DSC00768 (3.8MB)

FILES IN FINAL DRAFT
(screenwriting software):
ROGER SCREENPLAY 1 (25KB)
ROGER SCREENPLAY 2 (18KB)

AUDIO FILES:
ONE (48.7MB)
TWO (64MB)

ROGER SCREENPLAY I
(by Wiggy)

The kitchen of a coastal cottage on a gusty night. Scary stuff! Windows rattle. A kettle steams, having just been boiled. There is a sense of awkwardness, reflected in the music. Under a pool of yellow light at the kitchen table, a digital audio recorder is glinting. Facing each other at the table, their backs in shadow, are WIGGY and ROGER.

Close-up on the recorder: it is recording.

Close-up on wall clock. It is 11.45. Close-up on window: it's very dark.

WIGGY shudders. He is a handsome man in his mid-thirties; attractive and serious. ROGER stares, breathes. Music now suggestive of heartbeats. WIGGY speaks first.

> **WIGGY**
> Shall we start?

ROGER
Whenever you like.

WIGGY
Can I get you anything?

ROGER
Such as?

WIGGY
Water.

ROGER
No.

WIGGY
Tasty titbit?

ROGER
(*affronted*)
No.

WIGGY
(*trying to lighten the tone*)
Saucer of milk?
(*laughs*)
Ball of string?

ROGER *gives him a pained look. He is a cat, of course. In fact, I probably should have mentioned this at the top of the scene — NB: Remember to go back and do that.* ROGER *is a cat. Otherwise, if* not *clear* ROGER *is a talking cat, the scene might be somewhat less interesting.*

WIGGY
(*abashed*)
Sorry.

WIGGY *attempts an encouraging smile, but* ROGER *is stone-faced. As well as being a cat, he is a bit of a bastard, to say the least. NB: Is this the right place to start the story? Yes, surely. Or possibly no. Oh God, I have no idea.*

ROGER
Can I just check? You're not going
to write this up like a screenplay?
I mean, in a screenplay format?

WIGGY
(*lying*)
No, I'm not. Why?

ROGER

I've read your other screenplays, don't forget. You
used to send them to Jo. We laughed like drains.
You go in for very self-indulgent stage directions.

WIGGY *rises above this, superhumanly. But what a nerve.*

WIGGY

So, Roger. Here you are.

ROGER

(*not really paying attention, bored*)
Yes.

WIGGY

A talking cat!

Note to self: Remember to make this clear at the top.

ROGER

Yes.

WIGGY

Would you like to tell me —
(*he falters, understandably*)
— something about that?

ROGER *has been thinking about something else. Close-up on* ROGER.

ROGER
(thoughtfully)
What do you say to Daniel Craig?

No one will believe this. But it did really happen.

WIGGY
(confused)
What do you mean: what do I say to him?
I've never met him.

ROGER
If this becomes a film.

WIGGY
I'm sorry?

ROGER
You can be very dense sometimes, Wiggy.
What do you say to getting Daniel Craig to do
my voice in the film, *if there's a film?*

WIGGY
Well, I hadn't really thought—

ROGER

(*interrupting*)

He's very understated.

WIGGY

Yes. Yes, he is. Famously.

ROGER

He's classless. I like that.

WIGGY

Yes.

This is exactly how the conversation went.

ROGER

Masculine.

WIGGY

Absolutely.

ROGER

Emotionally reticent.

WIGGY

Yes, but—

ROGER

He'd be perfect.

WIGGY
(*laughs*)
Except that you sound nothing like Daniel
Craig, Roger. You sound like Vincent Price!

ROGER *jumps off the table, landing softly on the stone-flag
floor, tail raised high. What a prima donna. He just can't
stand it when* WIGGY *gets the last word on anything.*

WIGGY
(*calling*)
Roger! Oh come on.

ROGER *looks round and makes a loud — and very pointed
— miaow.*

WIGGY
You've got a great voice, Roger!

ROGER *pushes through the cat-flap and leaves. Music climax.*
WIGGY, *sighing, switches off the recorder. Windows rattle.*

*Outside, the garden gate creaks and bangs in the wind. Beyond
is the cry of the sea.*

Note to self: Do this again; still not working.
Remember it's quite unusual that a cat is talking.

Difficult to get the proper distance on this when you've got so used to it. Formatting quite professional-looking, though. So that's encouraging, at least.

JPEG DSC00546

The picture shows an unremarkable moggy-type cat — tabby and white. White face and bib. White paws. Tabby back, tail and ears. Slightly hefty. Harmless-looking. He is lying in the arms of a tall, striking woman in a grubby artist's smock, her long brown hair lifted by a sea breeze. She is smiling. At her feet is a small brown terrier of attractive appearance whose tongue is hanging out. Behind is a flint and brick cottage — the name SHINGLE COTTAGE visible on the lintel.

ROGER THOUGHTS
(by Wiggy)

Where to start? The crazy thing, or Jo? Well, Jo. Obviously, Jo. I mean, where the hell is she? You can't just disappear! There I was, Coventry, Belgrade Theatre. God. Four o'clock-ish. Thursday afternoon. Just going on in the second half of the matinee of *See How They Run*. 'Call for you,' they said. Alice, the ASM. I didn't have to take it, but I did. Thank God I did. It's Jo, sounding weird. 'Wiggy,' she says. 'Wiggy, please come. It's Roger. You've got to help me take care of him.' Or something like that, but I can't be exactly sure. Well, I was a bit distracted! We're building up to the bit where Jeff says, 'Sergeant, arrest most of these vicars!' and it's important to concentrate. And my big sister is calling me at work to talk about looking after a cat? 'Jo, I'll have to call you later,' I said. I handed the phone back to Alice, and made my entrance through the French doors – just in time, I might add.

Anyway, after the curtain, I called the cottage, like the decent chap I am, but no luck. It kept going to voicemail. Ditto the mobile. I left a couple of messages. 'Orfling Two calling Orfling One' — that's our code to each other — well, that's been our code since Ma died and left us on our own when I was still at school. Jo's Orfling One, of course. And I'm Orfling Two. But she didn't call back. Alice said afterwards that she'd tried to ask Jo what the problem was — they met when Jo loyally visited the show when we came to Worthing (the cottage isn't far from there) — but she said it was hard to make out anything distinct from the phone because of all the laughter in the theatre — some of which, I'm pleased to say, was generated by yours truly. What did the *Coventry Bugle* say? Well, thank you for asking. I believe it was, 'Will Caton-Pines manages to make the thankless part of Clive, the husband, almost believable.'

Anyway, back with Jo, I kept trying to call her for the next couple of days. At the end of the week, I just drove down here. Orflings must stick together, and anyway it was the end of the run. And of course there's no sign of her — or even of mad dog Jeremy, who's normally so glad to see me. I say 'of course' there's no sign of Jo — but why do I say that? There's no 'of course' about it! *Where is she?* Even as I drove up the muddy lane from that bloody village it felt all wrong. Her car sitting on the soggy grass across from the house. Big gate open. Back door unlocked. Handbag in the hall. Jeremy's collar and lead hanging from the peg, next to the one where she usually keeps the spare keys for the next-door neighbour. Mobile phone plugged into the charger in the kitchen. Heating on. 'To do' list on a chalk board — do this, get that, take care of whatever. It felt like she'd just popped out. It *still* feels like she's just popped out — and I've been here four days. Don't know what to do, apart from write this.

I did ring the police yesterday, and a detective called Sergeant Duggan came and took a statement. I showed him all round the house, the shed, studio, little cellar with historical smuggling connections and whatnot. Took him down to see the beach. Pointed out the fine view along the coast to Littlehampton. We knocked next door, but that chap's always away — lives mainly in France. Jo's only met him once since she's been here. I explained how the two cottages used to be one house, built around 1750, and how Ivor Novello used to visit the one next door in the 1930s, when it belonged to a star of the musical theatre. I suppose I got a bit carried away telling him about next door – all the parties and whatnot. I shouldn't have bothered! You can always tell with police when you're giving them 'too much information', because they stop writing it down. My big mistake was asking him in a jocular way whether anyone had ever said to him, 'Sergeant, arrest most of these vicars!' He didn't have a clue what I was talking about.

I explained that Jo had called me at the theatre to say 'Look after the cat' – and he was quite cross with me then, because what she said suggested she was intending to go away. But she hasn't *gone away*. What it *feels* like – I didn't say this to Sergeant Duggan – but what it *feels* like is that she's been taken by aliens. And it also feels like the abduction happened within the last half-hour. I keep expecting the J-Dog to come trotting past, asking for a pat. I keep expecting chairs to be still warm when I sit down – and sometimes I get a real start when they *are* warm, Roger having just hopped down when he heard me coming. A really perverse cat, Roger. Since I first got here, there's been this sort of scratching noise from the wall with the fireplace in it, and you'd think — as a cat — he'd be desperate to investigate. But he's lain there calmly in Jo's high-backed armchair, just a couple of feet away from the source of this suspicious noise, swinging his tail and ignoring it absolutely.

The policeman asked if he could look at Jo's mobile — and of course, that was clever of him, so I said yes. But although it was still plugged into the charger, it turned out to have sort of died. And when he picked it up, he said 'Agh!' and dropped it (it was all sticky, he said). Anyway, he reckoned I should take it into Worthing to see what could be retrieved from the 'SIM card' (God, I hate all that kind of stuff), and he helped me use rubber gloves to put it in a plastic bag.

I have to admit it: he was much more observant than me; I suppose it's the training. In Jo's studio upstairs, he found a half-finished watercolour of Roger, and heaps of sketches for it all over the floor. I hadn't noticed. He also asked about a pair of binoculars and a notebook, with times noted down in it, right by the window next to an old, cold mug of tea. 'Tuesday, 10.05. Next-door garden. Partial.' That kind of thing. Jo being a birdwatcher was news to me. But the big window in the studio would have been a good place to do it. Lovely view across to the English Channel and the horizon. He asked if anything significant had changed in Jo's life recently, and I said, 'Well, yes. Roger,' and he seemed quite annoyed with me again for not saying anything about Roger earlier. He made a note of the name and drew a circle round it and asked for a surname – which was when I realised he thought Roger was a lover or murder suspect, so I quickly explained that Roger was a cat, and he crossed it out. So I didn't explain she'd only had Roger a few months – took him on when her old Chelsea Arts Club chum Michael died in Lincolnshire, falling downstairs. Likewise, I didn't draw attention to the way Roger had definitely made himself at home here. He was sitting in the lane as I approached in the car; when he saw me coming, he just stood up, stretched, and trotted indoors.

Now this is the crazy bit. Woo-hoo. Right. I mean it, this is absolutely crazy. Maybe I shouldn't even write it down. But all right, I was sitting at the kitchen table last night, drinking some of Jo's impressive stock of cheap pink plonk — which is disgusting, a bit like drinking melted lollies, but I was bloody desperate — and Roger was clawing at the back door, wanting me to open it for him. And I suppose I was in a bit of a trance. I mean, it's very unsettling not knowing where Jo is! I keep testing the phone line; I've been in touch with everyone I can think of; I've checked her computer and her diary, which felt really awful, really *wrong*. But I have to do these things, don't I? I don't know where she is! I didn't say this to the plod, for obvious reasons, but I've also checked all the grass in the area for tell-tale scorch marks, because in my opinion alien abduction is emerging as by far the most likely explanation. So anyway, I'm ignoring Roger, like I said, and he's saying, 'Miaow, miaow, miaow,' at the door.

Maybe I imagined it. Maybe I did. But what happens is this. He suddenly jumps up on the table, sits down in front of me, puts a paw over my glass and says, distinctly, 'Let me out.' I look at him. I feel a tingling in my head. I look at the paw. He doesn't move it. We look into each other's eyes for about ten seconds. And then he jumps back down on the floor and claws at the door again, saying, 'Miaow, *let miaow*, miaow, miaow, *LET ME OUT*.'

AUDIO ONE

'In your own time,' says Wiggy. He sounds quite upper-class. I can't imagine why this is a surprise, but it is. I picture Wiggy as a feckless type, of course. An actor, in silly farces, in provincial theatres. He went to a good school. Floppy hair, I shouldn't wonder. Mustard-coloured corduroys at weekends. From internal evidence, this recording must date from at least a week after Wiggy's first so-called 'thoughts' about Roger — but there is no dating whatever on these documents; as files, they were all saved on the same date in December when Dr Winterton sent them to me, which is quite unhelpful. As soon as I can, I will check when *See How They Run* was last playing at the Belgrade Theatre in Coventry. Thus far, it is my only clue.

The quality of this recording is not of the best. Background noises sometimes obtrude. And when there is any sudden sound, such as Wiggy coughing (of course, he *smokes!*), the recorder reacts, and Roger's words are rendered temporarily less audible. Also, Roger sometimes swallows his words in a miaow — possibly deliberately. As King George VI says in that highly successful film *The King's Speech*, a couple of stammers 'thrown in' serves to remind the British people — to whom he broadcasts — that it's really him. I have no doubt Roger operates on the same intelligent and witty principle with his occasional miaows. As you will see, Roger is an astonishing individual. But I said I would refrain from editorialising. I genuinely intend to do my best.

The following is a faithful transcription of what can be clearly heard in the file marked 'Audio One'. If it is helpful to know this, Roger *does* sound a bit like Vincent Price. Essentially, it is Roger's life story, told in his own words. I have long since ceased to care that every aspect of this monologue — the teller; the telling; and above all, what is told — is technically utterly impossible.

'This is like *Interview with the Vampire*,' says Roger.

'Really? I never saw it,' says Wiggy.

'Shame,' says Roger. (He says 'Sha-a-a-me' in a striking feline sing-song.) 'The parallels are so amusing.' ('A-mewwsing', ditto.)

Wiggy says (without thinking): 'Oh God. You're not a vampire, are you?'

A long sigh from Roger. One sympathises with his problem here. 'No, not a vampire,' he says, quietly. And then he begins.

'I was born in 1927 in the East End of London, and before you tell me that's impossible, Wiggy' — you can almost hear the tiny mechanism in Wiggy's brain doing the mental arithmetic — 'may I remind you that a cat talking into this recording device is impossible enough, but I think you will agree that it is nevertheless definitely occurring.

'So. I repeat, I was born in 1927 in the East End of London, close to the Roman Road market. My mother was very beautiful, and very young. I never knew my father, but that's pretty standard for cats so please don't bother trying to read much into it, although I have to admit that a sort of father-fixation — with its associated rejection issues — has arguably been a theme of my whole life. Have you read much Freud, Wiggy?'

'Er, no,' Wiggy says. He sounds a bit startled by the question, and you can't really blame him. In any case, Roger clearly isn't interested in discussion.

'My brothers and I learned to scavenge and hunt,'

he goes on. 'We played at fighting, as all kittens do; we made adequate progress. There were four of us all born together — Alf, Arthur, me and little Bill — but we were reduced to three when my brother Bill was killed by a carthorse when we were six months old.'

There is a pause. Wiggy starts to ask, 'Are you all right?' but Roger resumes.

'I must say,' he says reflectively, 'I thought Mother would be more affected by the loss of little Bill.'

You can hear how shocked he was by this; how hurt by extension, of course, at how little his mother would have grieved for any of her offspring, including him.

'I was just a year old when I met the Captain. In the intervening six months I had often visited the spot where little Bill had met his end, and I had sometimes been aware of a large black cat watching me there. I assumed that one day this cat would expect me to fight, and although I wasn't looking forward to it, I was big enough, so it was bound to happen. In the cat world you don't really choose who you fight, you see. But although we met each other in the conventional way — backs arched, tails erect, teeth bared, circling with our claws digging into the dust – he disarmed me by saying, "You miss him, don't you?" In my surprise, my back dropped down, my tail flopped. No one had ever said anything like this to me before. I was confused. "Your little brother," he said. "It was a senseless way to go."

'And then he walked off, and I followed him. It was the turning-point of my life. If I hadn't followed the Captain, what a different story would be mine. A straightforward cat's life around the Roman Road, circa 1930. I'd have survived (if I was lucky) to about the age of six. I'd have fathered dozens of kittens. I'd have used up all my so-called "nine lives" in mundane ways, such as recovering from drunken blows, losing my tail in some old housewife's wringer, getting stuck for weeks in a garden shed. Such was the everyday fate of the other members of my family, certainly. Although I never saw them again, I found out later that Alf was run over by a number 30 bus when he was two, and I heard that Arthur made it to five years old but was rounded up and taken to Battersea Dogs Home, where the story goes that he was gassed. I don't know how anyone can be sure of that. But it's sad to think your last sibling was lost to you in 1932, the year the Mars Bar was first produced, the Lindbergh baby was kidnapped and the Sydney Harbour Bridge was opened. I very much doubt you can imagine it.'

Wiggy, realising something is required, makes some sort of hopeless mumble. Perhaps he's making a mental note of the interesting fact about the Mars Bar.

'What I do know,' resumes Roger, 'is that Mother had two more litters and then collapsed and died in Victoria Park in 1932, under a favourite tree. I suppose every animal from a fatherless background thinks the same as me, but in all my years I've honestly never seen a more beautiful cat than Mother.'

Wiggy takes advantage of a natural pause. 'I expect I'm being thick,' he says. He clears his throat. 'But when this other cat – this Captain – spoke to you, do you mean the way you're speaking to me now? Or was it some sort of cat language?'

Roger is incensed at his stupidity.

'Of course it was cat language! I just told you, I was only a year old! I'd spent my kittenhood in the slums!'

Wiggy is clearly mortified. But I must admit

I'm rather glad to hear him on the back foot like this. He really is out of his intellectual depth with Roger.

'Don't be like that,' Wiggy says. 'It's just that you seem to take it for granted that you can *talk*.'

'I don't take it for granted at all. You're the one with the problem.'

'No, I'm not. Look, how do you explain——?'

Roger interrupts. 'Wiggy, if you can't get past the fact that I can talk, perhaps I should stop.'

'No, please. I'm sorry. You're very touchy.' Wiggy laughs, and attempts a joke. 'I mean, you know. Keep your fur on. You were following the Captain.'

'I know I was following the Captain! You don't have to tell me I was following the Captain!'

There is no sound in reply from Wiggy. In fact, you will be pleased to hear that Wiggy does his best not to provoke Roger again for the rest of this recording. The incendiary expression 'Keep your fur on' is thankfully never reprised.

'So, yes. I followed the Captain. I made my choice. I expect I was inwardly proud that he seemed to have sensed something special in me. I had no idea what was in store. He led me into an old warehouse, all the way silent. There were so many things I wanted to ask him, but I knew he would speak only when we were safely alone together. "Here we are," he said, when we were finally inside. He spoke in a weary way. I didn't know then how old he was. I didn't know how many times he had gone through this process before. "You're wondering why I picked you out," he said. "Let's just say I had a hunch about you." I looked round. From the darkness, I was sure I could hear the far-off groaning of an injured cat.

"'Is there someone else here?" I said. I hoped I didn't give away how anxious I was.

"'Yes," he said. "I'll explain to you later. If there *is* a later."

"'What do you mean?"

"'Well, here we are." He sat down in front of me, his huge yellow eyes looking right into mine. Being captured by his gaze filled me with a strange mixture of terror and blissful joy. He leaned forward and said, very quietly, "Has anyone ever talked to you about cats having nine lives?"

'And then, before I could say anything, he lashed out at me with massive ferocity, slashing my throat. My blood gushed out, fell like heavy rain to the ground; I stumbled and fell, weakly, feeling the pulse of my heart pumping my tiny young life out of me as I lay there, helpless. I remember that I felt surprise — utter surprise — but no resentment, no anger. In some ways, I didn't really mind that I was going. I thought briefly of Mother, but then remembered — without rancour — that she probably wouldn't miss me very much. A happy memory of little Bill came back, which made me smile. And then my mother's special smell filled me up — filled me with almost unbearable comfort — and I succumbed to death.

'When I woke, I was desperately thirsty and my eyes hurt. They were like rocks in my head. Obviously, my main feeling was confusion — but these physical sensations were powerful too. My paws felt as if someone else's had been tied on top of my own. My tail was so heavy, I could hardly lift it. The Captain was watching me as if he had never moved. How long had I been dead? He pushed a water bowl towards me, and I drank every drop from it. He didn't speak, and I was too frightened to break the silence. Yet I had no urge to escape. I trusted him. He had just killed me — hadn't he? I had felt myself die. And yet I trusted him. After all, here I was, alive! My throat appeared to have healed itself. The blood on the floor had dried. Whatever had happened, somehow the Captain had it under his control.

'For the following few days, he brought me food and I got stronger. And then, on the seventh day, he said "Follow me", and led me to another part of the building. This time, I didn't care if he knew I was afraid. "Captain, please," I said. "I need you to explain what's happening." But he shook his head and we made our way into the darkness, in the direction of the groaning I had heard when we first came in. He stopped on the edge of a pit about fifteen feet deep. It was too dark to see to the bottom, but I could detect movement down there, and smell an overpowering stench of animal decay. I could hear cracked and laboured breathing, and the unmistakeable squeak of rats – a sound that drives any cat crazy with loathing and bloodlust. "You'll understand soon," he said – and knocked me in. I screamed as I fell; I also screamed as I landed. Lining the bottom of this pit were the decomposing bodies of at least a dozen cats – their loose fur horrible under my paws, their dying breaths still hanging vilely in the air. Rats swarmed round me, climbed over me. I struggled to breathe, lashing out in all directions. "Help me," said a voice close by, and then there was a dreadful, feeble wailing.

'I was down there for six whole days before I expired. My death was caused by a combination of dehydration, asphyxiation and rat-induced dementia. This second demise had none of the emotional consolations of the first. In fact, it was the worst of all the deaths. It's no wonder that the Captain always placed the pit second in the sequence. As he explained to me in the fullness of time, very few cats rose out of the pit and made it to their third life – let alone made it eventually (as I did, so amazingly) to their ninth.'

Roger stops. 'You look confused, Wiggy,' he says.

Wiggy evidently shrugs his answer. 'Nngh?' is all I can hear. He lights a cigarette and sighs. One can hardly blame him for his slowness to grasp what Roger is telling him. I must admit that, in his shoes, I would have struggled to come up with a meaningful response myself.

Finally, with an effort, he takes a drag on the cigarette and says, 'Nine lives, then?'

'It is quite a big idea to take in, I suppose,' says Roger.

'It is, yes.'

'Just cling on to that idea.'

'Of the nine lives?'

'Yes.'

'All right, but—'

'Just think about what a strange belief it is — *every cat has nine lives*. Why do humans say that? Where did you get such a bizarre idea? Why do you pass it on? The Captain used to say how typical it was that while all humans seemed to know the saying about cats having nine lives, not one of you had stopped to find out what it really meant — so you applied it, pathetically, to the famous luck of cats in surviving mundane accidents.'

He pauses. Wiggy swallows. He manages a feeble laugh. 'Ridiculous,' he says.

'In fact,' says Roger, 'as the Captain explained to me, *every* cat literally has the capacity within him to survive eight deaths.'

'Right.'

'Up until, say, two thousand years ago, all cats had powers unimaginable to the average cat today. The species has been vastly diminished by time and domestication. In the modern world only one cat in a million has the character, the spirit, the sheer indomitable life force to fulfil that universal feline destiny of nine lives as part of a conscious programme of self-completion. I am that one in a million. And if I seem quite pleased with myself – well, so would you if you'd survived the shit I had to go through. My initiation with the Captain was long and merciless, a symphony of pain and despair. And it got worse and worse. What one has to take into account is that the risk of failure – the risk that I would die for good the next time the Captain killed me – kept growing, exponentially.

'The Captain loathed all the killing, he said – and even from the point of view of the poor little street cat on the receiving end, I believed him. But I grew quickly to understand, as he did, that there was no other way of finding out whether I was The One. If you'll excuse the pun, this was the ultimate process of elimination. After cutting my throat and then leaving me to die in the pit, he went on to hang me, drown me, brain me—'

There is a little whimper from Wiggy here.

'Gas me, burn me and poison me – each time

having to prepare himself for an even greater likelihood that I would not return. When I recovered from the final test, I found him bent over me, weeping. He thought I hadn't made it.

'He thought you were dead?'

'Exactly.'

'Wow.'

There is a pause.

'But you weren't dead?'

'No.'

'Wow.'

'Wiggy, look, I'll explain it again.'

'Would you? Cheers.'

'He had killed me eight times.'

'Yes.'

'I survived each time.'

'OK.'

'Meaning that I'm the cat that *literally* has had nine lives.'

'Right. Like every cat has nine lives, kind of thing?'

'Except that most cats nowadays die once and that's it.'

'Got it. Got it. I think I've got it.'

Roger waits. Wiggy makes a 'Huh!' noise of exhalation.

'I'm a very special cat, Wiggy,' says Roger. 'That's the bottom line here.'

'Well, I know that. You can *talk*.'

Roger sighs. 'Yes, I can talk,' he says, flatly. This is clearly as far as he's ever going to get, explaining things to Wiggy. He goes back to the story.

'I wish I could remember everything he told me. The trouble is, once someone has shown you a convincingly different way of looking at the world, it's hard to remember how you saw it before. If it helps (but I suspect it might not in your case, Wiggy), the Captain was a classic Nietzschean. According to his world view, he and I were both *Überkatzen*, and it's true that once you are an *Überkatze*, the feebly simple one-bang-and-you're-out mortality of others – especially of the weakling human – is impossible not to be impatient with. In the process of finding a companion for himself, the Captain had sacrificed literally hundreds of cats, over the course of forty years. Scores and scores of them had not survived the initial slashing; a mere dozen or so had raised his hopes temporarily by coming out of the pit. But not a single one before me had got even as far as life number five! All this killing had made the Captain sad and weary and disgusted, he said — but it was the sense of perpetual let-down that had injured his spirit the most.

'"With every cat I had hope," he explained. "I thought, perhaps this one will have what it takes! But they *died*. One after another, they *died*. And in the end, their pathetic weakness made me sick. Can you imagine it, Roger? Losing all compassion? Feeling only fury and dismay?"

'I felt that I could. But I said, carefully, "I don't know."

'"Think of little Bill," he said. "I know you loved him. His death was senseless. But be honest. Having survived as you have done, over and over, eight deaths that were each of them far worse than his, what do you really think of him now?"

'I thought of Bill's little broken body. Of the kitten who had been so sweet and beloved. Of my sense of loss; the shock of his sudden departure from this world. And then I said, with perfect candour, "You're right. Little Bill? What a *pussy!*"'

There is a pause. Wiggy (thankfully) says nothing. And then Roger laughs. It is a shriek of a laugh, that raises all the hairs on the back of my neck each time I play it. 'Your face!' he says. And then he laughs and laughs, and then, abruptly, the recording comes to an end.

JPEG DSC00021

This picture, in black and white, shows a man standing in a patch of bluebells in dappled light. He has a handsome face. Big ears. He holds a lit cigarette. Beside his leg sits a cat – the same cat as in the first picture, the one I assume is Roger. Roger is pressing his head against the man's calf in what looks like an affectionate way. I wonder if the man is Michael, the one who died in Lincolnshire and bequeathed Roger to Wiggy's sister Jo? No, it can't be. It's from much longer ago. The man's trousers are post-war; he looks a bit familiar. The quality of the picture is fuzzy, as if it had been printed on soft paper.

JPEG DSC00768

Again, black and white. Again, the picture quality suggests a fairly ancient date. 1960s? Two cats together: one is the supposed Roger cat, the other a massive black tom with a handsome head. The black cat is lying down, stretched out on a patch of long grass in sunshine; the Roger cat lies on his back, his legs in the air, his head resting on the black cat's abdomen. They are both relaxed. If they were young men instead of cats, you would assume they had been for a drink and a swim after their final examinations, and that there was an ancient teddy bear called Aloysius lying half hidden in the grass. Behind them, little is in focus — a tree is casting shade across the bottom left-hand corner of the picture. Still, you can make out bushes, trees and an Elizabethan chimney.

I looked at this photo several times before noticing, right in the foreground at the top of the picture, a hazy horizontal shape. It makes no sense — being presumably some distance off the ground, and too close to make out properly. I narrow my eyes, searching for detail. It looks like a pair of brogues, heels together, toes pointed out.

ROGER NOTES
(by Wiggy)

Roger has been tearing stories out of the papers!
I left the *Telegraph* on the kitchen table last
Thursday, and then went out into the garden.
When I came back in, there were holes in it, not
to mention really deep scratch marks in the
table-top. I suppose it's my own fault for cutting
out the crossword for him every day. It set a
precedent. But I thought it was pretty reasonable
when he first made the suggestion. After all, it's
true what he said: I don't do cryptics. I don't have
the right kind of brain.

Of course, he's giving me the silent treatment
still. Not a single coherent word for a week. The
bastard. All miaowing. Miaow, miaow, miaow. God,
it sounds so sarcastic when it comes from him. It's
like it's in inverted commas. What sort of cat is
he, anyway? He *never* dealt with that scratching
noise, did he? In the end, it just stopped. Anyway,
back with the cuttings: the big Silent Act meant

it was pointless asking him what these stories were that he was so bloody interested in. He's done it again every day since, as well, as if he's looking for something in particular. So today I had one of my Wiggy Brainwaves. I secretly bought *two copies* of the paper from the village shop – and hid the second in the fridge. Which might sound a bit odd, so I should explain it's not *me*; it's Roger. The thing is, Roger, for all his mental brilliance, hasn't been able to work out a way to open the fridge! I've started keeping my wallet in there, just to be on the safe side. I put Jo's phone in there too (still in the bag), after I realised Roger had been playing with it in the garden, and had nearly lost it under a bush. I really *must* take that phone to a phone shop soon and see what can be done.

Anyway, back with my cunning plan: I left the first *Telegraph* on the table as usual, and went out for half an hour for a pensive smoke beside the sea. Then I came back in, to find the paper on the table in the usual tatters, and quickly carried both papers to the downstairs loo. It took a while to work out exactly what had gone, but in the end it turned out he had torn out three stories. Which were:

1) A light-hearted news item about the statistics concerning various bizarre fatal domestic accidents last year in the UK (caused by teapots, dressing gowns, place mats, trousers).

2) A story about an East End gangster who had apparently taken his own life by jumping off the roof of a car park near the 2012 Olympic Stadium.

3) The obituary of some obscure academic from Cambridge.

No idea what to make of any of this, and as I said, I can't even ask at the moment. Miaow, miaow; miaow, miaow, miaow. He really is a bastard, Roger. He *won't* tell me what has happened to Jo – or he has to tell me his whole so-called life story first, which will take several bloody years at the rate he's going. And then he clams up for a week and just does cryptic crosswords *in his head*, making contented purring noises to let me know how clever he's being. Sorry to get worked up, but how the hell do you talk to a cat like Roger? Whichever approach you take, you feel like a total idiot. On the one hand, you can't say normal cat things like 'Ooh, what's for *your* dinner tonight? Is it a bit of lovely fishy-wishy?' He's the feline equivalent of Stephen Fry, for God's sake! On the other hand, what if someone came in and I was saying to the cat, 'Oh, Roger, I forgot to tell you, I bought you that copy of Shaw's *Man and Superman* you asked for. Where would you like me to put it?'

If Roger never spoke again, would I mind? It's a toss-up. It's certainly a lot more peaceful round here when he's in 'proper cat' (or what I call PC) mode. But when he's not talking, I feel I'm making no progress and might as well be dead. I don't know what to do with myself. I did have a look through Jo's binoculars yesterday, and saw hardly any birds at all, so what a waste of time. Puzzling, though. Whatever Jo was watching for, she saw it virtually every day — in fact, this is quite interesting, on the day she called me, she made a note of seeing it at about 3.30 in the afternoon — which would be just before she called me at the theatre! The handwriting is quite shaky, so she must have been excited. Also, thinking about it, wouldn't it have been almost dark by then? Well, that means it can't be birds! To be honest, this makes me even more keen on the aliens theory.

Maybe that's what she kept seeing . . . a flying saucer! Maybe she just had time to pick up the J-Dog and *Whoosh!* — up they both went, off across the dramatic coastline of Littlehampton and beyond to the Isle of Wight. (Although she did have time to call me first, which slightly ruins that scenario.)

Talking of scenarios, I had another go at a bit of proper writing at the weekend, but it's hard to get a grip on it somehow. Ever since Roger suggested Daniel Craig to play him 'in the film', I can't help picturing him dressed in a shiny designer suit, running along the top of a train as it goes round really tight corners coming out of Istanbul. He's got quite an idea of himself, hasn't he? I play along with that Nine Lives story of his, but I don't *care* about any of this stuff — why should I? He could be making the whole thing up. And meanwhile, I learn nothing about what's happened to Jo — *nothing*. That policeman came back today and asked whether I'd had the mobile looked at yet. I think he was quite surprised when I got it out of the fridge to give it to him, but he didn't say.

ROGER SCREENPLAY 2
(by Wiggy)

A cottage by the sea. Peaceful. WIGGY *strolls into kitchen, lights cigarette, fills kettle, casually opens fridge. Bond-type action music as* ROGER *explodes out of fridge, lands on* WIGGY'S *shoulder and delivers a devastating range of blows.* WIGGY *drops to his knees.*

WIGGY
(*yells*)
No! Roger!

More blows. NB: ROGER *makes no cliché squalling cat-fight noises. He is silent, focused, methodical, assassin-like. (This makes it more scary.)* WIGGY'S *arterial blood spurts and pours on to kitchen floor.*

WIGGY
(*naturalistically*)
But how did you open the——?
I thought you didn't know how to open the——!
Get off!

A final coup-de-grâce swipe to the throat. WIGGY *keels over, dead.* ROGER *jumps down on to the floor. He stops, raises a paw and admires his bloodied claws with a secret smile. He looks back at the lifeless body of* WIGGY *and the fridge door swinging open.*

ROGER
(*with classless, masculine understatement, over the shoulder*)
Nice Smeg.

AUDIO TWO

The second recording has a different ambient sound. As we discover, Wiggy and Roger are in a borrowed flat near to Russell Square in London. Cars and lorries pass outside. The pavements are evidently very busy, too: groups of young people can be heard. Dogs bark. Sirens pass. It's a winter afternoon. As will become apparent, Roger has persuaded Wiggy to take him on a trip down memory lane, and they have gone together to London.

'Ready?' says Wiggy. He sounds a bit tired and

tetchy. Perhaps it's been a long day. 'Might we get as far as Jo today, Roger? Where did we leave your life story last time? Around 1928? How fast can you do the next eighty-something years?'

There is a pause. Wiggy tries another tack.

'Had it changed a lot?' Wiggy asks. 'I could tell you were shocked when it turned out they'd built the Olympic Velodrome directly on the site of the Captain's special place.'

Again, Roger doesn't speak.

'Do you miss the Captain?'

Roger laughs. 'No,' he says. He laughs again. And I apologise for saying this, but *anyone else but Wiggy* would realise that this is an intriguing answer, and would follow it up. Wiggy, frustratingly, does not.

'Why did we have to see that car park?'

'Just a theory.'

Wiggy thinks for a moment. He is evidently making a connection to the car park suicide from the papers! Each time I listen to this recording, I pray again: *Don't mention the cuttings from the newspaper, Wiggy. Knowing the contents of those three stories torn out by Roger from the* Telegraph *is your single advantage right now.*

You will be pleased to hear that, for once, he makes an intelligent decision.

'Will you live for ever, Roger?' he asks.

'That was what I asked the Captain,' says Roger. 'When my ordeal was over, all those years ago.'

There is something quite mechanical in the way Roger picks up the tale where he left off. It makes you wonder: how many times has he told it before? What is his purpose in telling it to someone like Wiggy?

'*Does this mean I will live for ever?* The very question I asked the Captain. *Does this mean I can never be killed again?*'

He's off again. 'After all, would anyone choose to have eternal life? One needn't read very deeply in the great myths and stories of the world to know the general verdict on eternal life – immortality is always discovered to be far more of a burden than a blessing. Living for ever deprives the spirit of hope and purpose. It also separates you from mortals in mainly tragic ways. Think of the Sibyl at Cumae – or, if you like, Wiggy, given your more limited range of cultural reference, think of Doctor Who. Of course, I didn't think like this in those far-off days of my youth. I hadn't read anything.

I didn't know anything. I was a rough-edged street cat familiar with just a couple of square miles of East London. But I knew enough to be afraid of what the Captain had done to me. After all, as a Nine Lifer himself, he was clearly not a happy cat. He did not rejoice in his own immortality, if that was what he had. It was clear that the only thing that gave him happiness was me. He was wonderfully proud of me. He had created a companion for himself. For a week or so, all he wanted to do was congratulate me, marvel at me, tell me the story of my triumphant nine lives again and again and again.

'We moved from the warehouse after a week or so. Why should the East End contain us? For the next ten years, in fact, we travelled. In the first instance, it was easy enough to get to the docks at Tilbury, to hop aboard a ship and leave London far behind. We both adored the idea of life at sea, and we had all the requisite skills for stowing away on board. When you think about it, any ordinary cat is good at making himself invisible, scavenging, defending his territory – and we were not remotely a pair of ordinary cats! I recall that we always encountered trouble at first from the pre-existing cat population, but the Captain was more than a match for them. On the first ship, which was bound for Cape Town, we were no sooner out of the Thames Estuary than we were cornered in the engine room by four big heavy cats. In my mind's eye, these cats had tattoos and thick accents, but I've always been a big reader so my imagination might be embellishing things a little. Anyway, I remember how I took several deep breaths, readying myself for a fight with these tough mariner felines. But the moment I started to yowl and spit, the Captain struck me in the chest to silence me, and hissed, "I'll take care of this."

'What happened next was simply amazing to watch, and requires no embellishment whatsoever. Soundlessly, he walked towards the four big cats, and sat down in the middle of their circle. They were confused (as was I!), but at the same time couldn't believe their luck. The Captain looked at the biggest of the four — the cat looked back. And then something phenomenal happened. The other cat started to edge backwards, and he also shook — as if he had lost control of every muscle — and I'm not lying, for a moment or so he sort of lifted off the ground. The Captain looked into the eyes of the next cat, which immediately edged back as well. I had my paws over my eyes — he was going to slash all their throats, wasn't he? He would kill them the way he had killed all those others! But he wasn't interested in killing them, it seemed. He just overwhelmed them, vanquished them, terrorised them, and they retreated, and we never saw them again — because (as I later realised) they threw themselves overboard. In my innocence, I thought they hid from us for the remainder of the voyage. I would sometimes remark to the Captain that we hadn't seen them since the encounter in the engine room, and he would say, "You're right!" — as if he couldn't explain it either.

'It was the grandest of grand tours. We saw art. We saw architecture. We read books, and learned languages. All this time, the Captain was teaching me to talk, to read, to reason, to memorise. Long sea voyages are excellent for all such projects of self-improvement, as long as there's a fairly stupid person (there usually is) in charge of the human stores. Oh, the reading! How we loved to read. The Captain with his Conrad, me with my Kipling and Robert Louis Stevenson. From Cape Town, we made for India. After India, we saw Egypt,

Italy, Greece. The Pyramids by moonlight. The Forum by moonlight. The Parthenon by moonlight. My best memory of all is of lying on a rocking wooden deck on a starlit night, in the Aegean, with the Captain reciting Tennyson's 'Ulysses' faultlessly beside me.

Roger is evidently so moved by the recollection that for a moment he almost turns conversational.

'It was Greece that captured my heart. Have you been?'

Wiggy starts to draw breath, but Roger changes his mind.

'It doesn't matter. It will have changed so much since the 1930s in any case. Have you read the Durrells?'

'Um—'

'We knew them in Corfu — well, they didn't know *us*, because we kept ourselves to ourselves, but we lived very happily for a while at all three of their villas. We borrowed Larry's books; we read some of his manuscripts. We even helped ourselves to some of Gerald's smaller zoological specimens. In the end, the Captain and I spent three whole years in the Greek islands, and it was the very best of times. I was coming of age, I suppose. I was finally beginning to understand – and enjoy – my freedom from normal mortal constraints. I'd been reading some fabulous travel writing. Mixing with top-notch people. And meanwhile everything inspired me. I loved the light in Greece. I loved the air. I loved the fish! And Greek cats were no match for us, those skinny things, so we never had a bit of trouble (the cats in the Forum are another story!). I was so very happy on the isle of Symi in the Dodecanese – which were under Italian rule at the time, of course, as you'll remember from your Hellenic history at school – that I hoped we would settle there for ever. I pictured us living in a cave and becoming a bit famous, maybe even the focus of a cult – something like St John the Evangelist on Patmos. But it was foolish to dream of such things. Because it was on Symi that the Captain started to reveal an unfortunate trait – a kind of psychotic possessiveness – which in the end made me anxious to move on, and meant we were never safe for long in any one place.

'At Symi, you see, something rather horrible occurred. The first of a series of horrible things. And I blame myself: I had ignored the signs. I had assumed the Captain was as happy as I was. A kindly waiter at a harbourside taverna would sometimes tickle me under the chin and fling me a piece of octopus. I thought it was nice of him, and I played up to it — scoffing the titbit and miaowing for more. His name was Galandis, and I stupidly mentioned him to the Captain. I even made the excited suggestion that we might want to settle down at Galandis's taverna, and be looked after for a while.

'The Captain pretended to be interested in my suggestion. He made me point out Galandis when we were sitting on the harbour wall one evening. The next day, when Galandis was feeding me, I noticed the Captain was watching. It all seems so clear to me now, but at the time I thought he was weighing up the idea of making our home here, so I was (what a fool!) quite pleased that he saw me purring and nudging at Galandis's ankles. Two days later, I arrived at the taverna and there was no Galandis. His wife was sobbing, people were shouting (they're always shouting in Greece, but this was different), and the church bells were tolling. The focus of attention was a black handcart dripping seawater on to the ground. I hopped up on the harbour wall to see what was in it; what was causing the dripping water; what was causing all this unseemly human grief. It was Galandis's body, of course. My sweet Galandis! He had drowned himself.

'The Captain joined me on the wall. "What a shame," he said. "That was your nice human friend, wasn't it? They're saying he jumped into the sea from his little fishing boat last night, and he had rocks in his pockets."

'"But why?" I said.

'"Who knows?" shrugged the Captain. "Sometimes humans just lose the will to live."

'Three more blameless Greek people, on three different islands, had to set the church bells tolling before it dawned on me that it wasn't a coincidence. The fat man from the post office on Samos; the hairy-faced woman on Hydra who sold honey; the fisherman's idiot son on Cephalonia with the public-nuisance shoe fetish — how peculiar that every time I got to know a human being, he or she immediately *lost the will to live*! I thought for a while that it might be *me* — that I somehow infected these people with despair. But it must have been the Captain. He was possessive; he was a classic psychopath (obviously); and he had nothing but contempt for the average human. However, I never had evidence that he tampered with any of them – not Galandis, not the cuddly postman, not the honey-lady or the fisher-boy. The only time I saw him interfere directly with a human was in 1933, when we were strolling through the temple at Luxor on a fine afternoon and an American woman decided to take a photograph of us. "What enormous cats!" she exclaimed and snapped the shutter. Well, the Captain wasn't standing for that. And it was as if we had rehearsed it. He ran to her. She bent to stroke him. He slashed her leg. She screamed and dropped her camera, which he knocked away, in my direction. Then he streaked off and I quickly lay across the camera, as if asleep, while the woman was helped away, hobbling and bleeding, by the native guide.'

Roger laughs. Wiggy, rather uncertainly, joins in. He obviously feels he should say something.

'That was quick thinking on your part,' he says.

'Teamwork,' says Roger, with a sigh.

There is a sense that this is the end of the

instalment. Wiggy scrapes his chair back (does he stand up?). But then Roger resumes.

'You're right. Perhaps we should stop now. But you must be wondering why I wanted to visit Bloomsbury, and I suppose I ought to explain.'

'All right.' Wiggy settles down again.

'It's about humans again. It began with — a boy.' Roger sounds different, suddenly. Less carefree; less in control. This is clearly not a happy story like the one about wantonly injuring a poor American tourist in Egypt. What if she got septicaemia? Roger doesn't care, and Wiggy doesn't think to ask. All Roger is concerned about is the 'boy'.

'He was an English boy in glasses and long shorts,' he says. 'And I spotted him at the Acropolis one day when I was on my own there. He was sitting on a piece of fallen masonry, in the midday sun, making an elaborate drawing of the Parthenon, working so hard on it that I was sure he was oblivious to everything else, certainly to me.'

'Why were you on your own? Where was the Captain?'

'On a bus to Piraeus. He'd gone to check the ferry times. We were leaving Athens the next day for Brindisi. The last words he said to me were—'

He stops. This is clearly emotional for him. 'Sorry,' he says.

'Roger, if this is difficult for you—'

'I'm all right. But ten years with the Captain – well, I realise now, they had made me . . . hubristic.'

Wiggy starts to say, 'What?' but Roger carries on.

'And where better to suffer for your hubris than in one of the greatest sites of ancient Greece? This boy – I was really drawn to him, you see. And I'd got used to the insane idea that the only possible bad outcome from interacting with a human would be a bad outcome for *him*. With his glasses and sketchbook and grey socks, he reminded me of those nice intellectual Durrells on Corfu. I felt sorry for him because he was sitting in full sun without a hat! As it happened, the Captain and I had recently spotted an old panama hat left in the dust near to the site of the Chalkotheke, and in my concern for him I didn't hesitate: I went and got it and dragged it over. It was possibly the nicest thing I've ever done for someone else. Well, how true it is that no good deed goes unpunished.

'The boy smiled, thanked me, and took the hat.

Then he poured some cool water from a flask into a little bowl and gave it to me. I lapped it up, and he stroked my head. "You're not a Greek cat, are you?" he said. I purred, a bit uncertainly. And then he uttered the fateful words. "Ah-ha," he said. "I thought so." What did he mean? Why the "Ah-ha"? Did he think I'd replied to him? Up to this time, I'm sure I had never spoken human language to a human. I'm positive I didn't speak to him! Yet somehow I did betray myself to that boy. It must have been clear that I understood what he said! Something I did gave me away!'

Roger's voice, when it rises, is a yowl of anguish. Wiggy takes a deep breath. But he knows better than to interrupt Roger's flow of thought.

'And then – oh it was vile,' Roger says, as steadily as he can. 'He picked me up by the scruff of my neck and said, "I've read about cats like you." Then he produced some string from his pocket, and before I could do anything, he'd put a running slip-knot around my neck and was pulling me away.'

'No!' says Wiggy.

'Yes!' says Roger. 'I yowled vehemently, and tried to fight him, but he held me out at arm's length; and that's how I was marched away from the

Acropolis, from the Captain, from all my happiness. No one lifted a finger to help me, despite my obvious distress. The Greek cats cheered. When we reached the bottom, the boy shoved me into a wicker basket; that same afternoon I was taken with a heap of other luggage to the port and put on a ship for England. In my panic, I kept repeating in my head those lines from Milton's *Samson Agonistes*:

> *Why was my breeding ordered and prescribed*
> *As of a person separate to God,*
> *Designed for great exploits, if I must die*
> *Betrayed, captived, and both my eyes put out,*
> *Made of my enemies the scorn and gaze,*
> *To grind in brazen fetters under task*
> *With this heaven-gifted strength?'*

'Gosh,' says Wiggy, impressed.

'Well, I admit, not *everything* in that passage fitted my exact predicament.'

'But the gist——?'

'Exactly!' Roger is pleased, for once, with Wiggy's grasp of essentials. 'Yes, what I've found so often in life is that recollecting poetry at key moments is all about the gist. Why, I asked myself. Basically, why was I made so special if I was going to end up in a cat basket?'

Wiggy makes a sympathetic noise.

'So there I was. Not eyeless in Gaza, at the mill with slaves, but defeated by the tiny buckle that kept the door of a simple wicker basket closed! I had no way of telling the Captain what had happened. I just had to hope he would return to the Acropolis and that somehow he would work out where I'd gone.'

'Poor Captain.'

'Yes.'

'And poor you, of course.'

'Thank you, Wiggy. I'm afraid I do think "Poor me", even though, on the voyage, I suppose I was treated well enough. The boy's parents were academics who had the best literary conversations I'd ever heard, although they were far too soft on Robert Browning for my taste. The boy was not neglectful of me – he just made me very anxious. I could hardly forget that he had *read about cats like me*. But here's the point. When we arrived back in England, we came straight to London, and I escaped – and came straight to Bloomsbury.'

'How did you manage it? The escape?'

'Oldest trick in the book, I'm afraid. Laundry basket.'

'And why Bloomsbury?'

'I suppose I only had one idea. Where would the Captain think to look for me? I'd worked it out on the voyage – he'd last seen me at the Parthenon, so the obvious place was the London home of the Parthenon marbles!'

'Oh, that's clever.'

'Thank you.'

'Are they anything like the Elgin Marbles?'

'The Parthenon Marbles and the Elgin Marbles are the same thing, Wiggy.'

Wiggy says nothing.

'So that was my thinking, for right or wrong, and the British Museum was my actual home both during the war and for a long time after. Even when all the objects were evacuated, I stayed put. I still visit as often as I can. I am proud to say that I know the layout of the Enlightenment Gallery better than I know the back of my own paw.

'The boy became an academic himself, in time. I followed his progress. He specialised in pre-Christian attitudes to animals – in particular, their relationship to the afterlife – as companions, and so on. He co-wrote a masterly work on the subject with a quite famous historian, and he also once wrote an affectionate piece in the *Times Higher Education Supplement* about the cat he had found at the Acropolis which later (or so he'd been told) lived wild in the British Museum, even throughout the Blitz. This cat had inspired him, he said. Well, as if I gave a damn about that! All I knew was that he grew up, he got older; in the fullness of time, he grew old. I, by contrast, have remained exactly the same, aside from becoming (if I may say so) much, much cleverer than he could ever be. But what he did, when he abducted me from Greece, was ultimately to draw to him the wrath of the Captain. He lives still, but it's a miracle, and I have reason to believe that he doesn't have long.'

MORE STUFF
(by Wiggy)

Sergeant Duggan brought the phone back with pretty extraordinary news. It had been urinated on, by a cat, *while it was charging!* Whoa. The effect was basically to electrocute the insides of the phone. Duggan said he'd never heard of anything like it. I said, truthfully, I bloody well hadn't either.

'Imagine!' he said. 'Why would a cat *want* to wee on a phone?'

I was just asking myself the same question when Roger happened to saunter into the kitchen, as if by coincidence, and the policeman (knowing not who he was dealing with) reached down and picked him up. It was, I have to say, a brilliant moment.

'Who's been a naughty cat, then? Who's been a naughty ickle cat?'

Roger looked at me over the policeman's shoulder. I waggled my eyebrows at him. He glowered. It was hilarious.

'Can't have animals at home. Daughter's allergic,' Duggan said, bending to put Roger down. I fleetingly wondered whether Milton ever wrote anything that covered the ignominy of that particular situation. I'd be very surprised if he had.

'Er, did they retrieve anything from the SIM thing?' I asked, trying to show a polite interest. I think the policeman realised quite a while back that I had no idea what a 'SIM thing' was.

'Ah, now,' he said. And he gave Roger a last pat

on the head as he straightened up. 'Now, because it's an iPhone, there's nothing stored on the SIM card apart from account data.'

Roger curled up on a nearby chair, as if unconcerned.

'All the interesting and useful stuff – things like messages, photos, voice memos, map references – they would have been stored on the phone itself, which, as we know, was destroyed, burned out—'

'By the peeing?'

'Yes, the inside of the phone was sort of electrocuted when it was unfortunate enough to come into contact with electricity and cat urine at the same time.'

I looked at Roger. He was doing a bit of grooming, but with his ears pricked up for every word. What a cool customer. However, he wasn't prepared for what the bloke revealed next.

'But fortunately, all is not lost!' he announced. And God, it was funny to see Roger's reaction. He fell off the chair.

'What? Oh *fuck!*' he said, aloud.

I suppose it slipped out. I gasped. Duggan looked at me, and said, 'What did you say?'

So I had to impersonate Roger, with his Vincent Price voice and everything. I laughed. 'Sorry, officer. I just said, "What? Oh *fuck!*" It's a funny family catchphrase, that's all.'

I could see he was confused, but he let it pass.

'You were saying all is not lost,' I prompted.

He frowned at me. 'Yes, well. Most people "sync" their phones with their computers. In many cases nowadays, it happens automatically when the phone is in range of the computer in the house. And if your sister did that, we can sync this replacement phone.' He held one up. 'And then we can find out at least what was on her other phone the last time she plugged it in. Do you see?'

'Blimey,' I said. 'So whoever peed on the phone – they didn't think of that?' I couldn't help rubbing it in a bit. I was enjoying seeing how this news was affecting Roger. His tail was thrashing about like nobody's business.

The policeman was surprised. 'I don't suppose he did it on purpose, did you, ickle puss, ickle puss, ickle puss?' He reached for Roger again, but Roger backed off.

'Can we do it now?' I asked. 'The syncing thing?'

'Of course,' he said. 'Shall I—?'

I said absolutely, and he was just going upstairs when his own phone beeped with a text message. He stopped to read it. And I'll remember the moment for ever, I think. Up to that point, I was still enjoying Roger's discomfort. It was great being *in on it*, if you know what I mean. He had hopped up on the table, and I was stroking his head like a normal cat-owner, saying to Roger in a normal talking-to-animals kind of way, 'The nice policeman's going to sync Jo's phone upstairs, Roger. This might clear up the mystery of where she's gone.' And he was pretending he didn't understand a word anyone was saying.

'Any news?' I said, when the policeman had finished reading his text.

'Not relevant to this, no. Sorry,' he said. 'Silly, really. We thought we'd just check whether this cat-peeing-on-a-charging-phone thing had ever been recorded before as part of, you know, "suspicious circumstances".'

I felt Roger's body go tense under my hands.

'And?'

'It turns out it has. Oh well. There's nothing original in this world, I suppose.'

Roger pulled away, jumped off the table and

strolled to the cat-flap — but waited to hear the end of the conversation before going outside.

'So you mean it *has* happened before?'

'About six months ago, apparently,' the policeman said. 'In Lincolnshire. At the home of some sort of artist who fell downstairs.'

An hour later, we had flicked through nearly all the contents of Jo's phone — and let's just say we had different ideas about what we'd found. *He* thought we'd found nothing! 'Oh well, it was worth a try,' were his exact words. What he'd been looking for, I suppose, was a name, a number, a secret lover, a villainous fancy man. So a series of pictures of the garden, taken from the upstairs window, with a large, unknown black cat in them — sometimes with that loyal dog Jeremy face to face with him — were of no interest whatsoever.

And then we looked properly at the last picture taken with the phone — a picture just of Jeremy on his own, the little J-Dog, Jo's beloved little Border terrier. At first glance, it had looked like a simple snap of Jeremy lying on his side on the gravel by the gate. But oh no, this was not a doggie having a lie-down in the sun on some nice winter's day. This was taken on the day Jo disappeared; the day she called me in the theatre; the day something really bad happened at this house. Poor little J-Dog was lying right beside the big five-bar gate that leads to the lane, and his face — well, his whole head, really — was crushed. The poor little thing was obviously dead.

The policeman and I went straight out to the gate and when we got there, I felt such a fool for having noticed nothing earlier. I've been here three weeks! And there were still traces of blood and dog hair in the hinge of the gate — about a foot off the ground, exactly Jeremy's height. Oh God, poor Jo. How she loved that J-Dog. I noticed Roger watching us from the garden wall as we examined the scene. It was easy enough to see what had happened. In the gravel — oh God. In the gravel, we even found some little doggie teeth.

'So the dog was sniffing *here*,' said the policeman. 'And then someone lifted the latch. Is it a heavy gate?'

I could hardly speak. I just nodded. The thing is, it's a *very* heavy gate, yes. And the way it swings open — Jo always said it was lethal. That's why we tended to leave it open. It had been open ever since I arrived.

With some effort, I walked the gate shut, to demonstrate. Dumbly, I signalled to him to stand back. One flick of the latch, and it swung open so fast and so violently that we both gasped.

'Jesus!' he said, catching it. 'She should have fixed this.'

'She was always meaning to,' I said.

So the poor dog must have been standing there, with his little nose right in the hinge of the gate, when someone lifted the latch. But why had he been standing there?

'Look at this,' said the policeman, bending down. 'He was deliberately lured.' And there it was. A bone, now stripped of all flesh, was wedged between the gatepost and the wall.

At this point, I'm sorry, I was sick.

'She wouldn't have done this herself?' he said.

'Oh God, no. God, no.' I fumbled for a tissue, and couldn't find one. I felt like crying: I kept thinking of the force of that gate swinging open, and the poor dog's head just cracking like a nut. It was as if I'd personally heard the noise; been there myself when it happened. The J-Dog had been dead before I got here! And all this time I'd been imagining he was safe, even enjoying himself, in a jolly spaceship, hovering over the Solent. Up on the wall, Roger was still watching, not moving.

The policeman made to leave. 'I'll find out if she took the dog's body to a vet's anywhere. This could explain why she left in such a hurry,' he said. 'Although it doesn't explain why she didn't take the car.'

He turned and gave me a searching look. 'It's a shame you didn't notice it before,' he said. 'And it's even more of a shame that you didn't do anything useful with that phone.' It was the first hint of unfriendliness in his tone.

'I'm sorry.'

'Mr Caton-Pines, I have to say this. You haven't done *anything* to find out what happened to your sister, have you?'

I thought of all the hours I'd spent since I got here, listening to Roger, thinking about Roger, *writing* about Roger, when I could have been focusing properly on finding Jo. In a way, what he said was true.

'I'm beginning to think you're not telling me everything.'

I didn't have to answer because I was throwing

up again. But *not telling him everything* — oh God, he was definitely right about that.

INTERPOLATION, WITH APOLOGIES

I promised I would allow the Wiggy files to tell their own story without any unwelcome 'editorialising', but something has happened that has made me change my mind. Yesterday, having reached a natural break in this batch of transcriptions, I left the cottage for the first time and drove to Norwich. I imagined I would go shopping for food, possibly catch an improving matinee at the arthouse cinema, and (if time allowed) spend a few moments at an internet café, checking on Wiggy's appearance schedule at the theatre in Coventry. In fact, I spent four hours at the internet café, and was so upset I had to come back at once. I now shan't bother with the file entitled 'Roger Dream'. It doesn't add much, except that in his dream Wiggy keeps being led to look at that peg in the hall — the peg that usually had the keys to next door but on which nothing was hanging when he arrived at the house. His subconscious mind has worked things out, even if he hasn't. *If the keys to next door are missing from the usual peg,* his exasperated inner self is asking, *what do you think that means?*

But that's enough of Wiggy's slow mental processes. The bare facts of what I discovered are these:

1: Will Caton-Pines (Wiggy to his friends) did appear in *See How They Run.* The *Coventry Bugle* review is exactly as he gives it. The play was on at the Belgrade just two months ago.

2: He is now at the centre of a gruesome investigation into the death of his sister. The noted watercolourist Joanna Caton-Pines, who had been missing for three weeks from her cottage near Littlehampton, was found in the first week of December in the cellar of an adjoining house, with the corpse of a dog whose head had apparently been crushed. Both she and the dog had been partly devoured by rats. She was alive when she entered the cellar but the dog was not. She died, says the preliminary report, of 'dehydration, asphyxiation and (possibly) rat-induced dementia'.

Her brother is the chief suspect, mainly because much of his behaviour is inexplicable. For example, he evidently showed signs of 'inappropriate amusement' when the mobile phone belonging to his sister was found to have been disabled. He also withheld from the police the fact that he had heard scratching from beyond the party wall for several days after his sister 'went missing'. Those scratchings were, of course, the sound of his sister clawing at the bottom of a heavy trapdoor to a cellar. After he eventually 'found' his sister's body, it is clear that he did not contact the police for at least three hours. In the interim, he evidently went on a bloody rampage, in which he bludgeoned a cat to death, beheaded it and incinerated its body in the garden.

3: The academic whose obituary Roger had removed from the *Daily Telegraph* was a Professor Peplow. He was eighty-two, and he appeared to have killed himself, using hemlock. In the 1960s he had co-authored a major work on the place of animals in ancient death cults with a Dr G. L. Winterton. Neighbours reported his agitation about repeatedly spotting a large black cat in the area. He left a note saying (these exact words) '*I have lost the will to live.*'

End of interpolation

PART TWO

Home

It was to a sad and comfortless house that I returned after cutting short my wintry sojourn by the sea. A film of dust had settled on everything during my absence; the windows looked smeary; Mary's favourite fern beside the front door had bent and cracked from thirst; meanwhile various damp items of unimportant post, many of them tactlessly addressed to my dead wife, littered the tiles for quite some distance along the musty hall, as if they had exploded through the letter-box. On what appeared to be a happier note, the dog seemed glad to be home. He scratched at the garden gate, and panted excitedly. This I found rather gratifying, until, as he was straining at the lead coming up the garden path, it dawned on me: was he expecting to see Mary? It was soon distressingly clear that such was indeed the case. Once inside, I'm afraid I grew quite impatient with him as he stupidly ran round and round, romping upstairs and down, barking and wagging his tail, pawing at closed doors.

'Stop it!' I said. 'Come here, Watson! Watson, stop it. *Come here!*'

I could not catch him. He raced in circles, scattering rugs, madly knocking against the furniture. It was only when he had searched the entire house three or four times that he was prepared to admit defeat. He crawled under a chair and glared at me with an accusing expression that was all the more tragic because, in happier times, Mary and I had often imitated it, for each other's amusement. 'Oh, *Bear,*' she would say to me (we had pet names for each other, I'm afraid). 'Bear, how *could* you?' And then she would pull the accusing doggie face, and we would both laugh. No wonder I couldn't bring myself to look at him right now. I deeply envied him, though, in a way. All this time, had he simply forgotten that Mary had gone? What a blessing such oblivion would be. Imagine if I could have forgotten all about the last couple of months myself — cheerfully bursting back into this house, calling for Mary, 'We're back! You were right not to come, it was freezing!' But imagine, also, the unbearable pain of remembering the truth; of having that happy oblivion freshly shattered. To re-experience the devastating news, overcome the disbelief once more and crumple yet again under the blow would be beyond endurance. It would be like dying twice.

I filled the kettle, adjusted the thermostat for the central heating, and considered the unpacking. Mary, of course, had perfected a very efficient system for unpacking, which rendered it quite painless, at least as far as her husband was concerned. The house, with all our possessions restored to it, would be back to normal within just an hour or so. I very much approved of Mary's system, because what it required of me, principally, was that I keep out of the way. I would retire to my study with the accumulated letters and bills, and re-emerge at dinner time to discover that the emptied bags and suitcases were already stowed in the back bedroom, the washing machine was halfway through a cycle, all the toiletries were back in their normal places, even the books were ready (in piles) to go back on to the shelves. Could I face the unpacking by myself? Could I recreate Mary's system, based on my tiny sideways knowledge of it? I looked at the heap of boxes and suitcases in the hall, and quailed at the sheer scale of the difficulty. In order to make life bearable at the cottage, I had taken with me (in the old Volvo) simply everything I could think of: cooking pots and radios and the laptop and *towels*, and a box of books, and a big blanket, and two phone chargers, a box of stationery, and all the dog bowls and all his balls and toys and his *special towel*. And on top of all the cargo returning to the house, I now had additional freight – acquired on voyage, as it were: the obligatory bag of left-over groceries such as porridge and butter, teabags and eggs – plus, of course, those time-honoured souvenirs of the outraged self-caterer: some minimally used washing-up liquid, a minimally used bottle of olive oil and a 99 per cent full extra-large container of very ordinary table salt.

Did I have the patience to cope with the organisational demands of all this? No. In that case (I heard Mary ask), would I prefer to unpack piecemeal over the next few weeks? No, Mary. I would not. I would hate that more than anything, as you very well know. Once clothes started spilling out of suitcases in the hall, I would have to move out and live in the car. But for heaven's sake, why was I even thinking about this? As a fresh wave of sadness broke over me, I had to sit down and swallow the emotion, while Watson — who might have been a real comfort to me at this point, had he made the requisite effort — continued to observe, accusingly, from under his chair.

It was Mary who'd had the idea of naming him Watson. At first, she'd liked the thought of saying to an enthusiastic puppy, 'Come, Watson, come! The game's afoot!' But it turned out to be a rather clever inspiration, and the name stuck. We both enjoyed finding 'Watson' quotations that fitted perfectly with the dog. My own favourite was: 'You have a grand gift for silence, Watson. It makes you quite invaluable as a companion.' Meanwhile, Mary preferred to quote the famous telegram summons: 'Watson. Come at once if convenient. If inconvenient, come all the same.' She even used to call it out in parks and woods, when Watson was off the lead. Mary never cared much what people thought of her. While others were trying to attract their own dogs by shouting, 'Monty! Monty, teatime!' Mary would be calling, 'Come at once if convenient, Watson! If inconvenient, come all the same!'

With the dog still watching me, I got up. In the hall, I found the box with his food and bowl. I opened it, extracted just the things I wanted, and (feeling guilty) closed it again. Guessing what was occurring, Watson came out from under the chair — but after wolfing down his dinner, he retreated once more. His grand gift for silence was not *quite* such an asset right now. I sat down again; I got up again. I took off my coat. Finally, with an effort, I put some tinned soup in a saucepan, and began to heat it up; while this was happening, I went to the gloomy study, switched on my computer and started to download (slowly) 216 emails. Back in the kitchen, I realised all the wooden spoons were still packed — so I managed without. Sitting down again, I sipped the soup and tried to start a list of things to do. Without thinking, I looked up at the wall, half expecting to see a board with GET THIS, DO THAT and TAKE CARE OF as the headings.

I looked for the peg where next-door's keys ought to hang. But of course neither of these items was in my own house. Although I could picture them quite clearly in my mind's eye, I had to accept that I had never, personally, seen them in my life.

I had, as yet, made no decision about Wiggy and Roger, but my instinct was strong: forget it. Try to forget Dr Winterton's file and all of its contents. What good could it do to dwell on this story? Was it even true? Why on earth was it sent to me? Was it perhaps sent in error? On the drive home, all the way, I had maintained a running internal dialogue. *Was Dr Winterton in desperate danger?* No, stop thinking about this. Dr Winterton means nothing to you. A smell of cloves, you said. That's all you remembered about him. A bit tough that poor Peplow had to die – although I have to say it was very classy of him to have chosen hemlock. *Why had Jo put her phone on to charge and then gone next door to hide in the cellar? Why hadn't she taken it with her?* You're right, this is a detail that makes no sense, but just don't think about it because there is no way you will ever know the answer. *Why did she think a next-door cellar was a good place to hide, anyway?* I can't imagine – especially if it had a heavy trapdoor that could make it your living tomb. *Imagine the sight Wiggy found when he opened that trapdoor.* No, don't. Don't ever try to imagine that. *You realise he heard the scratching for several days? If he hadn't been such an idiot, he might have saved her!* Don't say that. Please don't think like that. *Roger said that the pit was the worst of all deaths.* You're quoting a cat now. An impossible cat, at that. So just desist. All of this story, remember, is based on the completely unacceptable and ludicrous premise of an evil talking cat called Roger that travelled romantically in the footsteps of Lord Byron in the 1930s and now solves cryptic crosswords torn out daily from the *Telegraph.*

At six o'clock the doorbell rang. It was one of the neighbours – Tony something. He and his wife have lived in the house next door for six years or so, so I suppose I really should know their surname by now, but I'm afraid I left that kind of thing to Mary. I picked up Watson and opened the door with him under my arm. Mary and I both had a horror of Watson running outside when the front door was open, so we made it a rule to pick him up.

'Alec,' Tony said. 'I noticed the lights were on.'

I realise I haven't mentioned my name before. I

do apologise. I suppose it was because this wasn't my story.

'Everything all right?' Tony asked. He and his wife Eleanor have been very solicitous since Mary died. It was Eleanor who called the ambulance on the fateful day. She looked out of an upstairs window and saw that Mary had collapsed in the back garden. Her heart had just stopped, they said. It just stopped. As I stood there with Tony, I realised I had never thanked his wife for what she did, or even talked to her about it properly. Did she think me very ungrateful and ill-mannered? Or did she understand that, when someone dies, there is so much to do, and facing people is the hardest part?

It was still very difficult talking to people. I certainly didn't want to face Tony right now. I didn't know what to say.

'Just having some soup,' I said. 'Come in?'

'No, no. That's OK,' he said, but he remained shuffling on the doorstep — which was annoying, as it meant I had to continue holding the dog, and letting all the newly generated warmth in the hall go straight out of the house.

'How was the coast?' he asked.

'A trifle bleak,' I said. 'Are you sure you won't—?'

'I was just checking. You're back a little earlier than you said.'

'Yes. I'd had enough.'

'Well. You must come round for supper.'

'Thank you.' I looked at the dog in my arms. I was hinting that I should like to shut the door and put Watson down. Tony thought I was hinting at something else.

'Bring Watson.'

'Oh. Thank you.'

He turned to go, and then made a decision to say something more. I tensed up. I was afraid he was about to say something nice about Mary. But he wasn't.

'Someone was looking for you,' he said.

'Really?'

Instinctively, I held Watson more tightly, but otherwise I tried to show no reaction.

'We told him you were away, but he said he'd come back.'

'Oh. Well, thank you.' I tried not to smile, but I felt – what was it? To be honest, I felt excited. A mysterious visitor? A moment before, I'd been advising myself not to think about the Roger file ever again, and now I was secretly thrilled at the idea of this man who had been looking for me. What if it was Winterton?

'Was he . . . quite old?' I said.

Tony laughed. 'Incredibly old!'

I laughed as well. 'A bit dusty?'

'Incredibly dusty!'

'Dishevelled?'

'Incredibly dishevelled, yes!'

He seemed relieved that I knew who he was talking about.

'He said he was a friend of Mary's?' he said, with that modern upward inflection that suggests a question.

'That's it,' I said. I sounded quite hearty, which indeed I was. Perversely enough, the idea of a visit from Winterton was cheering me up.

'Apparently she worked with him on some project at the library.'

'Exactly,' I said. 'Some project at the library.'

He went back down the path and I shut the door. Then I put down the dog and laughed. Watson looked up at me with a quizzical air and wagged his tail, but I could hardly explain to him why I was so happy that the game was afoot; I didn't remotely understand it myself. Surely I didn't want to know *more* about the evil Roger? In the end, just to say something, I resorted to Mary's standard address to Watson, whenever he came back dirty from digging in the garden.

'Ah,' I said. 'You have been in Afghanistan, I perceive.'

Three days were to pass before Dr Winterton called on me. Perhaps he wanted to give me time to finish my unpacking — which turned out to be such a lengthy and demoralising process that I loved Mary all the more for the way she had stoically undertaken it so many times on my behalf. In the interim, while I waited for his visit, I tried to adopt a normal domestic routine, but being at home brought me closer than ever to my sense of loss. In the evenings I tried to watch television, but quickly gave up: everything touched me too deeply. Nature programmes, detective dramas and, worst of all, the news — everything mercilessly underlined the same theme: it was all death, death, death, and all entirely unsupportable. Polar bear cubs starved in the snow, prostitutes were stabbed in urban underpasses, old-age pensioners opened the door to teenage psychopaths armed with screwdrivers. The only recourse was to watch quizzes; but, sadly, those were impossible, too. Mary and I had watched *University Challenge* together, and she had invented a game whereby we would shout answers to the science questions in unison, and keep a running score of our (random) successes. Over the years we grew rather good at identifying types of mathematical question, and would take it in turns to shout 'Minus one!' — which more often than not (odd, but true) was the correct answer to the seemingly meaningless questions involving x and y. We laughed a hollow laugh at the astronomy questions; we were seriously competitive on history and literature; she was shocked by my terrible ignorance of art; we were both hilariously bad at identifying great composers from even their most famous compositions. 'Giotto!' I would say, regularly, to the art questions. 'Haydn!' she'd say to anything musical. Not long before she died, there was a week when Minus One *and* Giotto *and* Haydn were the correct answers to starter questions. We laughed and laughed. It was the triumph of hope over ignorance.

Speaking of literature, since Mary had died,

there were two lines from *Hamlet* that I found I couldn't stop thinking of. One was 'How all occasions do inform against me', and the other was: 'And a man's life's no more than to say "One".' I know it's fashionable to think that Shakespeare was not personally bereft when he wrote *Hamlet* (or that he didn't need to be), but I am positive, from that second line, that he was. Since Mary died, I have looked at people bothering about ridiculous things and I simply cannot bear it. How can they be ignorant of the fact that – in a second – we are gone? Any sort of cruelty or stupidity dismays me. And as for being conscious of the fragility of existence, one morning, as we walked to the newsagent's shop, a cyclist on the pavement shot past Watson, narrowly avoiding him, and instead of yelling in outrage I just went to pieces. I had to sit on a bench at the bus stop and hold the dog in my arms until I stopped shaking. Here is the truth of life's fragility: one moment you are a witty female senior part-time librarian of fifty-three, clearing weeds from the side of the garden path, and the next you are nothing but clay. One moment your heart is beating in your breast; the next it is a mass of bloody muscle, inert and dead.

One moment you can say the words 'I am'. And the next, you have no first person, no present tense, and no entitlement, as a subject, to act on verbs of any kind.

In the end, while I waited for Winterton, I decided to visit my old colleagues at the library. I felt I had already left it too long. I also thought the familiarity of the building might be comforting. But I should have known better. Revisiting a place of work nearly always makes you feel like a ghost. Well, when you feel like a ghost already, it is the greatest folly; and at every hurdle, I wanted to turn back. At the turnstiles, I found that there was a new security person; on the membership desk, a new assistant. Awkwardly, I explained to both of them who I was. I then had to wait while a humiliating phone call was made, and then apply for temporary membership! 'I ran the periodicals department for thirty years,' I said. 'I officially left only at Christmas.' But it was like speaking into a void. Once I had breached the walls, the stately marble catalogue hall felt more like home, thank goodness, but it was also stuffy (far too warm after the cold outside), and smelled overpoweringly of furniture polish and body odour (as I suppose it always has). As I looked round, I started to feel faint. I wished I had worn a lighter coat. Avril, the deputy librarian, greeted me warmly, but was then called away to deal with a student having a battle with a photocopier. I asked after my old periodicals assistant, James, who is now in charge of research services; unfortunately, he was in a meeting. So I was just wondering why I had put myself through this unnecessary psychological ordeal, when Mary's dreamy colleague Tawny happened to come along. To be honest, I had forgotten about Tawny. She was someone I had quite happily let slip from my mind.

'Tawny,' I said, and smiled hypocritically. 'How are you?'

I had always felt sorry for her on account of her owlish name — presumably the proud handiwork of irresponsible hippie parents. As Bertie Wooster famously remarked, there is, from time to time, some raw work pulled at the font.

'Alec! Awww. I was going to call you.'

'Oh?' I said.

Tawny had a sing-song sort of voice and wide eyes, and looked at you with a funny pursed-lip expression, like a kitten in a classic Disney animation. She had hair down to her waist, no make-up, and wore ballet pumps even when it was snowing. She was about forty-five years old. It used to drive Mary absolutely insane to work with her.

'Awww, I'm glad you're back. Awww, how's Watson?'

'Thank you, he's very well.'

She pointed a finger at me.

'I,' she said again, 'was *going to call you*.'

'Well. That's nice.'

'Have you got time to come and see?'

'See what?'

'What I was going to call you about,' she said.

I had promised myself not to risk going into the great reading room on this first, experimental return to the library. But now here we were, suddenly, in Mary's old domain – through the heavy swing doors, and into that perfect, hermetically sealed world of panelling and high windows and book dust and polish (and BO), and soft, continuous keyboard clatter. Over the years, the usage of the room had inevitably changed – from being a silent reading room, it had become a silent writing room. But its seriousness had survived the transition. Where many other campus libraries had become more like internet cafés, our great reading room was a place of intense, solitary learning. Mary had been ideally suited to her position here, presiding over so much heightened mental processing. Others might have been intimidated by it, but not her. Down each side of the room were the individual, lockable carrels that she could, at her discretion, allocate to research students and academics. It had surprised me to find out, when she first assumed her position, that not all students aspired to a carrel. I would have thought that having a tiny private panelled room of one's own within the library, with a bookshelf, lamp and desk, would have been any studious person's fantasy environment. But the rental fee was perhaps off-putting; whatever the cause, they often stood empty. Mary had told me that, once in a while, she would take a key to an unused carrel and lock herself inside for a couple of hours – 'Just to get a break from Tawny,' was what she used to say.

It was to one of the carrels that Tawny now led me. She held the key.

'Now this is really *strange*,' she said, in a whisper. 'We think it must have happened the weekend before Mary— Oh.'

She stopped. She couldn't say it, so I had to say it for her. It is the common lot of the grieving, I've discovered, to spend half your time saving other people's feelings.

'The weekend before Mary died?' I said, helpfully.

'Yes.'

I braced myself. I looked around. I didn't know yet what she was talking about. She had said the words 'It must have happened'. But what could happen here? Nothing had 'happened' in this reading room, aside from some gargantuan efforts at mental application, for about a hundred years. We had stopped outside carrel number seventeen, which I now faintly remembered was the little private space that Mary had joked about retreating to. Tawny turned the key, but I almost stopped her. Was I up to this? What if there was something in here – something personal to Mary – that would break my heart afresh?

'The thing is,' Tawny said, very quietly, 'the caretaker *said* he had seen a cat prowling about in the library, and he'd tried to catch him. But of course he never expected this.'

'A *cat*?'

'Shhh,' she said. I had forgotten to whisper. Some

of the readers looked round. We looked back at them, and I weakly gestured an apology.

As if to compensate for my outburst, she lowered her voice still further, and turned her big wide eyes to mine. 'We don't know how he got in,' she said. Her voice was so low that it was little more than aspirated mouthing. 'But he's on the CCTV. He's huge. Anyway, there's a bit of a smell, so you'd better—'

'Tawny, could you hang on a minute—' I said, but it was too late. She had opened the door.

'Oh my God,' I said. I stumbled back.

'Alec! Quick, oh, sit down. I'm so sorry. Wait here, I'll get someone.'

'No, no. Stay,' I said. 'Oh my God.'

I held on to the door jamb and tried to make sense of the scene inside the carrel, holding my hand over my face. The best way I can describe it is this: imagine you had placed a small, orderly panelled room in a jungle clearing and come back a week later when all the larger wild beasts had taken turns frenziedly tearing it to pieces, slaughtering inside it, and treating it as a lavatory. That's what this little carrel looked like inside – it had been both savaged and defiled. The walls were slashed and splintered, papers were torn and scattered, books looked as if they had exploded, blood was spattered in flying arcs. The smell, of course, was cat urine; and you could almost hear the echo of the feline shrieks and yowls that must have accompanied such a violent attack. *How big was this cat?* It was hard to believe that any animal smaller than a bear could have caused such horrific damage. There were claw-marks on the walls a good six inches across. And to think that all this violence had been done – in a way – to Mary!

'It's this bit that freaks me most,' Tawny said. She pointed to the drawer in the desk, which must have been locked when the cat got in. The area around the drawer was cut and slashed so badly that splinters and chips had flown off. Grimacing, Tawny pointed to where, embedded in the shattered wood, there was a large claw, its end coated in dried blood. It had evidently been dug so deeply into the desk that the cat had not been able to withdraw it.

'I know I'm being stupid,' she whispered, 'but it's as if it *wanted to get into the drawer*.'

'What's in there?' I said.

'Nothing. It's empty,' she said, and drew it out to show me.

Tawny decided I had seen enough. She shut the door again, and we moved to the corner of the reading room, where we could speak a little more loudly. One thing above all I needed to know.

'Did Mary know about this?' I said. 'Oh God. Tawny, *did she see this?*'

'We think she did,' said Tawny.

'Oh my God. Oh, Mary.'

'Actually, I'm sure she did. It was on the Monday morning, you see. Do you remember, I called you and said she had gone home, not feeling well?'

Of course I remembered. Mary had died later that day.

'This *must* have happened over a weekend, you see; and I remember she took the key on the Monday morning and came down here, and I was getting on with something and not really paying attention, but I'm sure she came straight back to the enquiries desk and said she didn't feel well. She had something with her — a small, slim book, I think, in one of those old university slipcases. She went up the spiral staircase behind the desk — I remember that, because she usually preferred to take the long way round to avoid it. She was gone for a while. And then she came back down and went home. And – oh, Alec. I never saw her again!'

A tear rolled down her face. I suppose she must have cared for Mary, working with her all that time. It had never occurred to me. I patted her awkwardly on the shoulder.

'She took away the key with her, which she shouldn't have done. But that's why we didn't find out what had happened in there until a few days ago, when Avril came up with a duplicate. The smell – well. We'd noticed the smell, of course, but we didn't realise it was coming from here. Some of the readers – well, you know what they're like.'

I nodded. I did indeed.

'Anyway, they're going to clear it out on Sunday when there are no students around. Did you see what it did to the *books*?'

I was still reeling. 'I can't take it in,' I said. There was no doubt that this carrel had been Mary's. In the debris, I had recognised her handwriting on some of the ravaged papers. But why hadn't she told me what she was doing in there? Why had she lied to me? Had Dr Winterton really been working on 'a project' with Mary? Why had she never told me? I was furious. What had she got herself into? And what, by extension, had she got me into, too? This destructive act had been done, without question, by a large and powerful cat! Oh God. Until this moment, it had been of no real concern to me whether the Captain existed or not. I could believe in him, or not believe in him: it was all the same. *It had nothing to do with me.* But now disbelief was not an option. For heaven's sake, I had seen one of his actual claws, violently embedded in a piece of venerable oak library furniture!

'Can you open it again, Tawny?' I said. 'I have to know what she was working on in there.'

Tawny pulled a face. 'I don't think you ought to touch anything, Alec.'

'I have to see,' I said.

'Ooh, I'm sorry,' she said. 'But technically I'm not supposed to show it to anyone. I just felt you should know.'

'Can I see the CCTV?'

'No, of course not!'

This was very frustrating.

'All right, where are the books from, at least?' I said. 'Do you know?'

'Oh yes.' Thank goodness, Tawny could see no

harm in telling me this. 'They're from the Seeward Collection.'

I closed my eyes and took a deep breath.

'Of course,' I said. 'Of course they're from the Seeward. Well. I see.'

The Seeward was a world-famous collection, donated to the library on the collector's death in the 1960s, and classified as 'arcana'. Since that time, it had been housed in a twenty-foot-square steel-mesh cage, deep in the library stacks. John Seeward is no longer a household name, but he had been a celebrated journalist-cum-'ghost hunter' in inter-war Britain – the sort of chap who made friends with (instead of running a mile from) self-styled diabolists such as Aleister Crowley. His collection had been used, in his lifetime, by the occult writer Dennis Wheatley. Seeward had collected books on ancient mysteries; also ghosts, witches, satanic rites and so on. In the library's online catalogue, books from the Seeward were indicated with the sensational (and not uncontroversial) symbol of a hand-drawn pentagram, complete with drip-marks – to suggest it had been drawn in blood on a wall. Many of us had, over the years, objected to the continued presence of the Seeward Collection in a respectable academic library, and argued quite forcibly for its removal or sale.

'Are you all right?' Tawny said.

I smiled. Unsurprisingly, I was a little distracted. She tried to comfort me.

'In the end, it's only books and papers that were damaged, Alec. No one was hurt, I'm sure. I think the cat must have just got locked in and gone berserk. An aunt of mine got back to her house in France once and found that a bird – a single bird on its own – had virtually trashed the place. It came down the chimney, they think. And before it died, it had pooed everywhere, broken a lot of my aunt's favourite things, and the worst thing was, it had *eaten all the spines off the books*.'

I had to think quickly.

'Is Julian in today?'

Julian Prideaux was the keeper of the special collections, and was very rarely seen. Mary and I despised him. He seemed to think that leaving an old threadbare cardigan (with a sprinkle of dandruff on it) over the back of his chair – sometimes for weeks on end – was a brilliant bluff, and that, discovering it there, we would all exclaim,

'Look! A cardigan! This means he can't have gone far! See, this dandruff is quite fresh!' How he kept his position had always been a mystery to me. He never once turned up to a departmental meeting; Mary and I had jointly decided he was the laziest librarian on the planet. I enjoyed asking Tawny whether he was in today. Tawny would know as well as I did that if it was a month with any letters in it whatsoever, the answer was probably no.

'I don't know, but I *shouldn't think so*,' said Tawny, choosing her words carefully. 'But look. Julian doesn't know about what's happened in there. Only a very few people have seen inside. We're waiting to get a better idea of the state of the books when we sort through everything on Sunday. Alec –' She turned the big eyes to mine, and seemed concerned. 'Alec, I think we should get you a glass of water, and then you should go home.'

I allowed Tawny to lead me to the staffroom, where I drank some water and left her there, promising that I was absolutely fine – the sight of the carrel had been a shock, that's all, I said. Also, I'd found the atmosphere in the library very stifling. Next time I came, I would remember to leave my coat in the readers' cloakroom in the basement! It was easy to forget to do this, I said, when you used to have an office of your own with coat pegs in it. She seemed satisfied, and she said goodbye. I gave her the impression that I would be heading home immediately. In this matter, I misled her, I'm afraid, quite deliberately.

By the time I did indeed leave the building, an hour later, my mind was spinning. I realised afterwards that in all my years at the library, I had never used it myself to search for information. Now that the occasion had arisen, however, I had every advantage. Comprehensively, I knew the ropes. Just to begin with, I knew that Julian's office was never locked, that it was accessible from Staircase B, and that even if (as aforementioned) Julian was the laziest librarian in the world, my dear wife Mary was the most conscientious. If she had borrowed books from the Seeward Collection, she would have left a record. Within a couple of minutes of larcenous (but surprisingly un-stressful) trespassing, I had obtained a list of the books she had borrowed. The loans had been carefully handwritten by Mary in Julian's ancient logbook – presumably in his absence. I quickly made notes of them all. The books mostly concerned funerary archaeology – which chimed with Winterton's already established academic interest in animals as ancient afterlife companions. A couple of the titles were in German – which I knew was a language Mary didn't have.

What captured my interest, however, was the last item Mary had borrowed. It was a rare item: a leaflet written by John Seeward himself, privately printed in a small edition in 1960. My heart sank as I saw the title. Oh, Mary. It was called *Nine Lives: The Gift of Satan*. Next to the title, Mary had carefully added a note on the book's size, pagination, and so on. It was typically thorough of her to do this. Such a slim pamphlet, after all, would be easy to mislay. What her notes indicated was that *Nine Lives* was of octavo size; it was a mere sixteen pages long; and it contained woodcut illustrations. Checking with the online catalogue for more details, I discovered that *Nine Lives* wasn't listed. This was frustrating. In my impatience, I tried entering key phrases such 'evil cat', 'cat evil', and 'evil talking cat', but it still did not come up. Fortunately, however, I knew that with a donated collection such as the Seeward, the card catalogue of the original classifier would have been preserved.

It didn't take long to discover that the Seeward card catalogue was, in fact, one of several dusty cases stacked behind Julian's desk. It had not been very respectfully preserved, it seemed to me: in the back of one of the card drawers there were stuffed some random bits and pieces — I saw a bit of old leather with a buckle on it, as well as some little plaster statuettes. Carefully, I riffled through the cards to find the right one. I then removed it from the drawer and took it to the photocopier on the fourth floor, where fortunately I saw no one I knew. I then quickly returned to Julian's office and replaced it in the drawer, but not before its unusual classification had caught my eye.

It was one I had heard about but never seen before. The great Public Library in Boston, Massachusetts, employed it in the nineteenth century. The other items, you see, had been catalogued according to the antiquated 'Beacham' system, with lengthy call marks, such as:

SEEWARD
W55a
Gruns 934

By contrast, stamped in red ink on the corner of the *Nine Lives: The Gift of Satan* card was the just one word, in capitals: 'INFERNO'. Its meaning, simply, was that it should be burned.

Winterton was not at all how I had remembered him. Yes, he was old, dusty and dishevelled, but my memory had conjured someone tall, gaunt and wraith-like, whereas Winterton was short and florid with an enormous head. He came to the house wearing a duffel coat, a gardening hat and some muddy wellingtons: I was hugely disappointed. For some reason, I had been picturing an impressive monk-like figure, possibly with long iron-grey hair, high-domed forehead and dark, beetly eyebrows: basically, I had been bracing myself for a cross between Christopher Lee in *Lord of the Rings* and the dementors in *Harry Potter*. But if Winterton looked like anyone at all in children's literature, it was actually Paddington Bear.

He arrived at dusk on the day I had been to the library. Watson barked at his approach. I took a deep breath, picked up the dog and opened the door in anticipation, and found Winterton outside, on the path, distractedly rummaging through an old Marks & Spencer's carrier bag. He looked up, stopped rummaging and smiled broadly. I was confused. Could this be Winterton? Or was it someone who had knocked randomly on my door, having lost his memory on the way home from his allotment?

He seemed to think he was Winterton.

'Hello,' he said, warmly. 'Alec, at last we meet properly!' he said, holding out his hand for me to shake. 'And Watson, my little friendy-wendy! How are *you*? How are *you*? How are *you*?' Watson, tucked under my left arm, started furiously wagging his tail.

I shook his hand. 'Winterton?' I said, incredulously.

'Yes indeedy,' he said. He went back to rummaging in the bag and found what he was looking for: a dog biscuit for Watson.

'Ah, here it is. Can he have it?'

I was taken aback.

'Oh. Yes. I suppose so. Come inside.'

Once inside, I put Watson down and Winterton held the biscuit above his head. Watson sat and gazed up at it, his tail wagging. He looked extremely happy.

'Do the trick,' Winterton said. And to my astonishment, Watson fell over backwards and lay still, as if he'd been shot.

'Good boy,' said Winterton. Watson rolled back on to his feet, took the biscuit, and happily trotted into the living room to eat it.

I couldn't help laughing.

'Good heavens,' I said. 'I can't believe he just did that.'

'Oh, that's a grand little dog. Mary let me teach him a couple of things. I can show you later if you like. He got that one in half an hour. Now, are there any windows open anywhere? Any doors? Can we block up the fireplace? We've got a lot of things to catch up on.'

Contrary to expectations, it was a jolly evening I spent with Winterton and the dog in the kitchen. We had a pleasant supper of soup and cheese; we drank red wine. There was just one problem: I had expected Winterton to explain everything to me (I had made a list of questions), and he didn't. He possessed all the knowledge; he had all the answers; but getting a straight reply from him on any matter turned out to be frustratingly difficult. Unlike Roger the cat, with his beautifully lucid (and rigidly linear) narratives, Winterton started everything in the middle. If he had been a book, I would have hurled him across the room. The trouble was not with his intentions, which seemed genuine. The trouble was with his brain. He had all the right thoughts, but not in the right order. This explained a lot, of course. Formerly, I had assumed that his lack of scholarly publication credits (other than the work with the recently deceased Peplow) was due to the nature of his subject area. What I now realised was that publication for Geoffrey Winterton, PhD (on his own), would have been a laughably far-fetched ambition. Coherent, organised argument was completely beyond him. No wonder he had turned to Mary for help.

'How did Mary get involved in your work?' I said, when we first sat down to our supper.

'She had a marvellous mind,' he said. He fed a sliver of cheese to Watson, who thereafter sat beside the table throughout our conversation, looking hopeful.

'I know,' I said. 'I know she did. But how did she get involved? When? What did she know?'

'She felt very bad about deceiving you.'

'I'm sure she did.' This was something I was still

coming to terms with. I was so shocked that she had been working with Winterton behind my back – good heavens, he'd apparently known Watson long enough to call him his friendy-wendy! But I wanted an answer to my original question. 'So when and how did it all start?'

'Mary said she'd found something for me in the Seeward, Alec. I need it. The Captain is closing in, you see. He got Peplow!'

I huffed.

'Can we come back to that?' I said. 'Please, for now, can you just please tell me how it all started with Mary?'

He looked at the ceiling. I think he was genuinely trying to focus on the question he'd been asked. Instead, he dropped a bit of a bombshell.

'Roger helped me put the folder together for you. We felt we owed you that.'

This was such a large piece of new information that I had to pursue it.

'I thought Roger was *dead*,' I said. 'Didn't Wiggy cut his head off?'

Winterton looked surprised. 'No.'

'But—'

'No, Roger's in fine form.'

'But Wiggy attacked a cat and did unspeakable things—'

'Oh, that! Sorry.' He laughed. 'Neighbour's cat. Neighbour's cat.'

He waved the back of his hand at me, as if to say it was nothing.

'I don't understand.'

'We're talking about the one that got killed at the cottage?'

'Yes.'

'Neighbour's cat.'

'But—'

'There was this black cat hanging around the house, you see. Went by the name of Inca — isn't that a good name? I've never been talented at naming animals. With a black cat, you see, you'd think of Blackie, perhaps—'

I interrupted. 'But the black cat hanging about *was the Captain*,' I pointed out.

'Oh no, no, no!' Winterton laughed. 'That wasn't the Captain!'

'The cat Jo had photographed on her phone wasn't the Captain?'

'No, no, no, no, no.'

I was baffled.

'Jo might have *thought* it was the Captain. She probably did think that. But it was just some neighbourhood black cat.'

'Really?'

'This is something Roger has remarked on before. He says there's always a black cat in any neighbourhood; he says once you plant the idea of the Captain with people, they start noticing black cats everywhere. But it was just this pet cat Inca that got attacked by Wiggy – in the wrong place at the wrong time. Completely innocent. Wearing a collar, he was; which is a pretty big giveaway. Little identity tag with a phone number on it, you see. But when Wiggy found Jo in that cellar next door, he was all worked up, wasn't he? Inca strolls in. Oops. Black cat, bang splat. Roger had made himself scarce, of course. He isn't daft, our Roger!'

I wasn't sure I wanted Roger described as 'our Roger'. Winterton seemed to be taking it for granted that I was part of this story already.

Looking back, I should have asked him then and there about Jo. Did he know why she had hidden next door? How had she become trapped? Why hadn't Roger told Wiggy where she was? But he still hadn't answered my original question.

'How did Mary get involved?' I asked again, steadily.

'They banned me from the library ten years ago, you see,' he said.

'Oh good grief!' I said.

It was time to adjust to the reality of this situation. I had been expecting Winterton to talk with the authoritative tones and narrative control of a story by M. R. James. I required a strategy. And the main thing was: I needed to stop asking open-ended questions.

'Did you meet Roger on the Acropolis?' I said.

'Oh.' He was a bit surprised by the sudden change of direction, but he answered me simply (which was a relief). 'Yes. Yes, I did.' He thought about it some more, and then added, 'Yes. I was very young.'

'Is his story about his nine lives true?'

'Oh, I think so. Yes.'

'Do you mind my asking rather abrupt yes/no questions like this?'

'No, no,' he said, cheerfully. 'It's probably best, you see.'

'Are you in cahoots with Roger?'

'Cahoots. Oh, um. Yes. I suppose so, yes.'

'Does he do your bidding?'

'Oh no! What? No, quite the opposite. *Quite* the opposite. I'm his creature, oh yes.'

'Does the Captain exist?'

'Oh, I'm afraid so.'

'Does he really have — I don't know, *powers*?'

'Oh my God, yes. Oh yes. Powers, yes. Sometimes he kills; sometimes people kill themselves. Oh yes, powers.'

'Is Roger telling the truth about their relationship in the files?'

'I don't know. What does he say?'

I was rather shocked that Winterton didn't know the full contents of the folder he had sent me, when I had studied it myself so closely.

'Mainly, that the Captain is jealous of Roger's closeness to humans, so he always arranges in some supernatural way for them to "lose the will to live".'

'What was the question again?'

'Is that the relationship between Roger and the Captain?'

'No. Nothing like it.'

'No?'

'Well, perhaps it used to be. But Roger hasn't seen the Captain for years and years, you see.'

'Does he look up to the Captain?'

'What? No.'

'No?'

'Not any more.'

'So?'

'He hates him. Basically, he wants someone to help kill him, you see. He was working on Wiggy, telling him the first part of the story, building up to the big stuff when he and the Captain were reunited after the war, but then it all turned nasty when Wiggy found out about Jo. So he'll have to start again now.' He thought for a moment. 'To be honest, he has already started again. On you. That's why he wanted me to send the file. It's all coming to a head, you see.'

I didn't like the sound of that.

'Can the Captain even *be* killed?'

'Ah. There's the rub.'

He gave me a significant look. He took a sip of wine. 'I'm enjoying this,' he said. 'Mary used to ask me a lot of questions too. At this very table. She would keep saying, "Don't ramble, Geoffrey. You're rambling!"'

He laughed at this pleasant memory. I closed my eyes, and he must have noticed.

'I'm sorry,' he said.

I waved it away. I wasn't going to share my agonies with Winterton.

'Look,' I said. 'This is what I really want to know.'

'All right.' He assumed a look of seriousness.

'It's a simple question.'

'OK.'

I took a breath.

'Winterton, were you responsible in any way for Mary's death? Did the Captain come here?'

He sucked his teeth, and pulled a face. I waited. And then he answered, quietly, 'Yes. I think he did.'

I put my head in my hands.

'I'm so sorry I got Mary involved,' he went on. 'Roger thought she was the perfect ally because she thought his story was all nonsense. We were getting very close to something, you see. If you help us now—'

I had so many other questions, but for the time being I could manage only one more.

'Have you ever heard of a publication entitled *Nine Lives: The Gift of Satan*?' I said.

The effect on Winterton was electric. He jumped up, and set Watson off, barking. 'No! How do you know about that? Have you got it? Where is it? *Is it here?*

That night it was windy and bitterly cold. Winterton left at around 10.30; Watson and I escorted him to the main road, where we saw him into a taxi. The bare winter trees were bending and rolling in the wind; light from the street lamps was both feeble and stuttering. We shook hands before he got into the cab. He really was a ridiculous little man, but if he had managed to evade the wrath of the Captain all these years, then there could be no doubt he had hidden depths. We quickly ran over the highlights of the plan we had made.

'Saturday at six,' I said. 'Back entrance, near the cycle parking area.'

'Right.'

'You have to be in position, because I'll only have a few seconds.'

'Right.'

'This doesn't mean I'm willing to be part of Roger's story,' I said.

He laughed.

'It's not Roger you have to worry about,' he said.

Back at the house, I returned to the kitchen and sat for a while at the table. The idea of Mary sitting right there and saying to Winterton, 'Don't ramble, Geoffrey' was both painful and comforting at the same time. I drank the last of the wine and patted Watson. Then I held up a treat above his head and said, with as much confidence as I could muster, 'Do the trick?' – and what do you know? He just looked up at the treat and whined, so I gave it to him.

As I blankly stared around the kitchen, I started to wonder whether I was any better than Wiggy, really. Was I missing vital clues staring me in the face, as he had done? After all, I now knew something quite important about Mary's death: when she had come home from the library on that Monday morning, she had known she was in danger. Working with the shambolic Geoffrey Winterton had attracted the attention of an evil cat – an evil cat capable of devastating a small room and its contents; an evil cat looking for a book written by a famous diabolist on the subject (presumably) of supernatural longevity in cats. Whether she believed in any of this paranormal stuff was immaterial. The point was: what had she done? Being Mary, she had acted. Putting two and two together from what Tawny had told me, I now believed that Mary had retrieved the Seeward pamphlet from the devastated carrel and hidden it elsewhere in the library. My wife was enough of a Sherlock Holmes fan to know that a library was the very best place in which to secrete a book. Behind the enquiries desk in the reading room, she had ascended the small, staff-only spiral staircase to the stacks above. From this I knew one thing for certain: she had not returned the book to the Seeward Collection.

Feeling I should do something, I looked up Seeward on the internet. The result should not have surprised me, but it did. I was astonished. Although he had been deceased for fifty years, Seeward was still very big news as far as the internet was concerned; thousands and thousands of followers were out there in the so-called global 'community' (what a wicked misnomer) of lonely, gullible nutcases.

'Shit,' I said, when I saw the scale of it. Watson looked sharply up at me, and I apologised.

It turned out that Seeward could be googled in umpteen ways – *John Seeward diabolist, John Seeward suicide, John Seeward collector, John Seeward immortality, John Seeward cat mastery.* Scanning quickly through the various sites, I found that opinion was divided on whether Seeward was a diabolist himself, or merely the cause of diabolism in others. What was generally agreed was that, having 'investigated' a famous haunted manor house in Dorset in the early 1930s for a newspaper feature, he had gone on to buy the property and convert it into a satanic weekend retreat for séances, devil-worship, pagan rites, licentious blood-quaffing and so on. Harville Manor became a byword for depraved goings-on, and after he moved in permanently after the war, he hardly ever left the grounds until the day in September 1964 when his lifeless body was found hanging from a tree in the garden.

Miraculously, there were photographs. There were press shots of Seeward with some of his celebrity house-guests, many of them elfin young men with emphatic side partings wearing exotic costume and eyeliner: presumably, Seeward and his friends made larky home movies — the sort of thing you see with the young Evelyn Waugh wearing an ill-fitting blond wig and pretending to puff on a pipe. In the photographs, I spotted Charles

Laughton and Elsa Lanchester among the guests;
also Gertrude Lawrence and other musical stars.
The Duke and Duchess of Windsor appeared in
pictures so frequently, you could believe they lived
there. But the most notable thing was the cats.
Seeward kept scores of them. In every picture there
would be half a dozen or more. In one disturbing
image, one of the elfin young men lay prone in an
orchard, absolutely surrounded by cats – about
fifty of them, arranged in ranks, and all apparently
on the point of pouncing.

In the end, I decided to make a file of these cat
pictures, and started dragging them off the
websites, hardly looking at them as I did so – and
then I spotted him – the Captain – and I shouted
'Yes!' Because, well, yes, there he was. I knew him
at once. In several pictures, Seeward was holding
the Captain in his arms (which can't have been
easy, given his size). 'Ahoy there, Captain!' began
one of the extended captions, but I didn't care; I
hardly needed the confirmation by now. A debonair
Seeward posed with his arms folded beside the
Captain sitting on a gatepost. With a cigarette
suspended from his lower lip, Seeward manfully
pushed a wheelbarrow with the Captain on board,

wearing a jaunty sailor's cap. The Captain sat in the bucket of an old-fashioned stone well in the grounds (imagine any other cat doing that!), while Seeward appeared to be turning the handle. The Captain challenged Seeward at chess, sitting on a table across from him, his paw resting on the White Queen, as if about to announce checkmate.

As I was scanning through the various websites, something struck me.

'Hold on,' I said. 'Of course!'

I opened the old 'Roger' file. That Elizabethan chimney I had spotted in one of the old photographs: was the picture taken at Seeward's house? Not remembering which jpeg was which, I opened both of the old black-and-white photographs — the first of Roger with an unknown man among the bluebells; the second of Roger and the Captain lazing in the long grass with the mysterious blur high in the foreground.

I whistled. There was no doubt about it. The unknown man with the cigarette was unknown no longer: it was John Seeward, celebrated ghost hunter and over-the-top cat fancier. And to judge by the dating of the other pictures I'd been looking at, this had been taken at some point in the 1940s.

The other picture in the 'Roger' file was – from the trees and the distinctively tall and curly brick chimney there was no doubt – taken in the garden at Harville. Studying it now, I noticed for the first time a date scratched in the corner of the negative – 3 September 1964. It sounded familiar, and for a good reason. This was the day that John Seeward hanged himself, leaving no note. The significance of this picture was revealed at last. This was the place he had done it. And while the cats lolled carelessly in the grass beneath, like Charles Ryder and Sebastian Flyte in the early, hedonistic chapters of *Brideshead*, the image in the blurry foreground was of Seeward's feet – the brogue shoes of a man dangling from a tree, on a beautiful late summer's day, in his own historic garden.

Watson was woofing and scratching at the study door, wanting to get out. I ignored him. I was lost in this search. Where had Seeward got the money to fund this lifestyle? Surely not from writing the occasional piece about haunted houses for the illustrated weekly press? There was no suggestion he had come from a moneyed background.

'*John Seeward wherewithal*' I typed into Google, but of course the word meant nothing to the internet.

'*John Seeward means*' got me no closer. '*John Seeward money*' I finally typed – and here, at last, was some information, though it was sparse and speculative. Evidently, Seeward's earnings as a journalist came nowhere near accounting for his seriously wealthy lifestyle; especially, it could not have paid for the collection, which was extremely valuable. Did the Devil himself subsidise John Seeward? You would be surprised by the number of sentient beings, capable of typing on a keyboard, who believe that he literally did. As far as many people were concerned, moreover, rural Dorset was virtually the Devil's second home. I found a news feature about Seeward, printed by a local paper after his death, in which various residents of the area attested to the 'goings-on' at Harville Manor, and complained of such things as spooked livestock and an oak tree splitting down the middle at midnight on a cloudless Halloween. They also complained about the cats. A Mr Corbett (aged sixty-five) alleged that there were rituals at the 'big house' in which cats were sacrificed and otherwise used in devil-worship. His own cat Tina had once disappeared for three months, and he was sure she was at Harville all that time. When she came back, she was never the same again. For one thing, she would sit staring at him, until he felt queasy. And she would also go into fits — foaming at the mouth and writhing and spitting — whenever the church bells rang out, or *Songs of Praise* came on the telly.

Few of the locals had ever seen Seeward, though. He kept himself to himself, especially after a scandal in 1952 involving a local schoolgirl. The case was never proved, but unsurprisingly the hoo-ha did nothing to make him less unpopular with his suspicious neighbours. For the last twelve years of his life he never left the grounds of Harville, and he allowed very few visitors inside. It was believed that he concentrated on reading and curating his impressive collection of arcana, and he also wrote the majority of his books in this period — books that he published privately and circulated secretly.

I checked back on my notes. When was *Nine Lives* written? It was published in 1960. I had to find it. More than that, I had to make sure it never got into the hands (or paws) of the Captain. But why should I be taking sides with Roger? Roger was an evil cat who not only deliberately ignored the sound of a woman dying in a cellar, but also fiendishly urinated on people's mobile phones to electrocute their insides and destroy incriminating evidence! What should I do? I kept thinking of poor Mary, caught up in this thing purely because she was clever and helpful and organised, and soft-hearted enough to take pity on someone like Winterton. And all this time, while I was trying to think, Watson was being incredibly tiresome, scratching at the study door and whining to be let out.

'All *right!*' I said, impatiently.

I let him out, and he raced to the kitchen, barking. I went straight back to the computer.

I had decided to have one last trawl on Seeward, and then go to bed. It was midnight by now, but it couldn't be helped. When I had finished my research, Watson would have his bedtime chicken treat and we would go upstairs together as we had done every night since Mary died. But before we did that, there was something on YouTube I hadn't viewed yet, and I had a feeling I shouldn't overlook it. It had come up when I was looking under '*John Seeward cat mastery*', and it turned out to be a five-minute black-and-white silent film, shot at Harville Manor in the 1930s.

It started with a makeshift theatre curtain rigged up in the garden on a sunny day. Seeward, smoking, entered from the left of the screen, and addressed the camera directly. Dressed very smartly in tweed, he had a slim figure and a light step; he might have been about to break into dance. There being no soundtrack, one could only guess at what he was saying. He indicated the curtain, and smiled. A breeze caught the curtain and Seeward waited for everything to settle before continuing. He evidently asked the cameraman if he was ready, then he walked to the right-hand side of the frame and ceremoniously (with cigarette clamped between his teeth) used both hands to pull a cord to open the makeshift curtain.

Watson was now barking frantically in the kitchen. He was getting quite annoying. I paused the film and called to him. 'Watson, stop it! I'm doing something!'

Seeward came forward again to explain, indicating what the curtain had revealed: a covered table with a cage on it. Inside the cage was a rabbit, cheerfully nibbling some lettuce. Seeward opened the cage, gently lifted the rabbit out and placed it on the table, while putting the cage on the ground. Then he looked to the right, and a large tabby cat jumped up. Seeward beamed at him, and spoke to him. He fondled the cat's ears, and stroked his fur. The cat pressed his face against Seeward's chest. All this time, the rabbit (sensibly) backed off; but it didn't have the requisite athletic skill to jump to the ground and run away. Seeward placed the rabbit facing the cat — about two feet away. And then, in the blinking of an eye, three things happened. The cat looked up at Seeward, who nodded. The cat's head made the slightest dart forward, as if the animal were hissing. And the rabbit fell back, dead.

Seeward then approached the camera, and went behind it; there was a wobble as the camera was handed over to him; then a second figure — presumably the cameraman, relieved of his duties — walked to the table, to examine the body. He was a pale young lad in agricultural attire, nothing like the sort of person normally seen at Seeward's house parties.

He looked astonished. He held the rabbit up by the leg. 'It's dead,' he mouthed, looking towards the camera. He pulled a face. Then three things happened very quickly again. The cat looked in the direction of the camera, then made the same small hissing motion as before, and the farm boy instantly dropped to the ground.

It was the end of the footage. I switched off the computer. There was a buzzing in my head, but otherwise it was quiet. I rubbed my temples and sighed.

It was only then that I realised Watson wasn't barking any more.

'Watson?' I called. 'Watson, where are you? Are you all right?'

There was no response. The house was silent. I stood up and went to the hallway. 'Watson? Watson, where are you?' I tried the kitchen – and he wasn't there. I tested the back door; it was locked. Where had he gone? Why wouldn't he come when I called him?

'Watson!'

Not a sound. No pitter-pat of claws on the floorboards; no woof; nothing. A shiver of dread went through me. Oh no. Oh no, not Watson. He's all I have.

'Watson, where are you?'

I stopped breathing and closed my eyes. In all my resolutions about finding Seeward's book, keeping it from the Captain and not trusting Roger further than I could throw him, I'd forgotten the most important thing of all: protect Watson. Protect Watson from everything: from evil cats using the hinges of heavy gates as a kind of nutcracking device; from evil cats who could cause instant death with a single application of overpowering malevolence. To lose my dog would be beyond endurance. What had he been barking at, just now? Why hadn't I paid attention to him? *What had he been barking at?*

'Watson!' I called, from the hallway. 'You're not hurt, Watson? For God's sake, say that you're not hurt!'

I stood still and listened. I could barely keep myself from weeping. How Mary had loved him. How we had both loved that little dog. How I needed him now, more than ever.

'Watson?' I tried to say it calmly. And at last I got a response.

'Alec, in here.'

I jumped in the air.

'Alec, in the living room. Don't turn the light on.'

It was a male voice, with a clipped, authoritative, unflappable tone. I stopped breathing. Who was it? Who was in my house? How had he got in? What had he done with Watson? He was telling me to go into the living room, but I wasn't obeying. Not because I was brave or defiant, but because I just couldn't move my legs.

I forced myself to breathe deeply. 'Where's Watson?' I demanded. 'What have you done with him?'

'Listen, we have to get out of here, and I've got a plan. Pack enough chicken treats for a fortnight.'

What can I say? It was Watson. And believe it or not, he sounded exactly like Daniel Craig.

PART THREE

Correspondence

From: Alec Charlesworth
Sent: Thursday 15 January, 4.25pm
To: William Caton-Pines
Subject: Roger
Attachments: Beside the Sea (folder) and HOME (file)

Dear William Caton-Pines,
This is a very difficult email to write. The long
and short of it is that I have heard of what
happened at Shingle Cottage, and much as I have
resisted becoming involved in the story of the
two individuals known as Roger and the Captain,

I find that I am now in it absolutely up to my neck. I have had to leave my house! I've had to move into a B & B near the station! It's really disgusting, too — a big damp patch on the wall above the bed, and an air-freshener on the landing so toxic that I have to carry Watson quickly to our room, for fear the smell will kill him. But I suppose that's neither here nor there. At least they let me check in after midnight, and have turned a blind eye to the dog. But you don't want to hear about that. Good God, I'm beginning like Winterton! You don't even know who I am yet! Rather than explain everything here, I have attached a folder and a file for you to read — some of which you will be familiar with, as it was written by you in the first place. I think it will make clear everything that's happened so far. When you have read it all, you will know everything that I know. Which means you will also be aware of many unanswered questions, and many frustrating gaps.

Before you read the attached, I feel I should apologise for some of my 'editorialising' in my account of the material in the folder 'Beside the Sea' — especially any observations detrimental to yourself. I believe I call you an 'idiot' on several regrettable occasions. I had no right to do this. 'Staggering stupidity' is a rather inflammatory phrase that leapt out when I was preparing the material to attach with this. On top of this, I noticed an unfounded and speculative reference to 'floppy hair' (you might be bald, for all I know), and also remarks such as, '*He really is out of his intellectual depth with Roger*' and '*For once, he makes an intelligent decision.*' I hope you can overlook such uncalled-for slurs. The plain fact is that I did find myself quite captivated by Roger. I can't help admiring him, even now. I think it was something to do with his educated love of Tennyson's earlier poetry and his profound aesthetic response to ancient cultural sites. Such intellectual elegance doesn't come along very often.

I send you all this with a particular purpose. I have a large favour to ask. Since my life is evidently in danger from talking cats with lethal powers who can penetrate academic libraries and engineer the cruel deaths of inoffensive terrier dogs — and since there is no one else in the world with whom I would dare even raise the subject of talking cats

— could I persuade you to act as my archivist? I realise I don't know your current feelings on what happened at the cottage, but please believe that I am appalled and horrified by everything that happened at Shingle Cottage to Jo and to the J-Dog — and to you, too, Wiggy (if I may). I intend that nothing like it shall ever happen again. If I could just feel that the record was being kept somewhere — by you — it would help me face all that has yet to be done. In short, will you be my friend?

Yours sincerely,

Alec Charlesworth, FCILIP

(Fellow of the Chartered Institute of Library and Information Professionals)

From: Wiggy [Caton-Pines]
Sent: Friday 16 January, 10.45am
To: Alec Charlesworth
Subject: Blimey

Dear Alec Charlesworth,
Blimey. How the hell did you get my email address?
Wiggy

From: Alec
Sent: Friday 16 January, 11.30am
To: Wiggy
Subject: Blimey

Dear Wiggy,
I'm afraid a certain cat leaked it to Dr Winterton.

From: Wiggy
Sent: Friday 16 January, 11.37am
To: Alec
Subject: Blimey, Jesus

Alec,
I need to think about this. Jesus. Bit of a bloody
shock. Raking it all up again. Wiggy x

From: Alec
Sent: Friday 16 January, 11.40am
To: Wiggy
Subject: Blimey

If you would just read the files, Wiggy. Please.
  Alec

From: Wiggy
Sent: Friday 16 January, 6.34pm
To: Alec
Subject: All right

All right, sorry, it took me a while. I've read them, and I have a question.

From: Alec
Sent: Friday 16 January, 6.36pm
To: Wiggy
Subject: All right

Go ahead. Anything.

From: Wiggy
Sent: Friday 16 January, 6.39pm
To: Alec
Subject: All right

Can your dog really talk, or did you make that up?

From: Alec
Sent: Friday 16 January, 6.52pm
To: Wiggy
Subject: Thank you

Dear Wiggy,
Thank you very much for reading the files. It means a lot to me. In answer to your question, no, I didn't make anything up. However, it might be significant that Watson hasn't uttered another word since we left the house on Monday night. Perhaps it was some sort of hallucination brought on by terror. If Watson did have a plan, he hasn't shared it with me. I've had to do all the thinking for both of us – and quite a strain it's been, I can tell you. It was just the way he said, 'Pack enough chicken treats for a fortnight.' If that *wasn't* Watson, it certainly sounded like the sort of thing he'd say.

I do so hope you decide to help, Wiggy. It took me the best part of two days to write the file entitled 'HOME', and it was only when I'd finished that I realised how alone I was with this story; how it *wasn't* a story, really, unless it had someone to read it. Tomorrow night Dr Winterton and I will attempt to purloin the Seeward pamphlet after the library closes. I am sure it contains the answer — otherwise why would the Captain go to such lengths to recover (or destroy) it?

Which reminds me: did Roger ever mention Seeward to you? Or anything about a 'Cat Master'? What did Winterton mean when he mentioned the 'big stuff' after the war? Why did Roger and the Captain fall out? It occurs to me that although the life-story tapes in the folder took him only up to his wartime experiences in the British Museum, he might have told you more — only off the record, as it were.

By the way, you never answered my question about whether you're willing to act as repository for the rest of this story.

Yours, Alec

From: Alec
Sent: Saturday 17 January, 4.30pm
To: Wiggy
Subject: Operation Seeward

Dear Wiggy,
Well, it's Saturday and I haven't heard from you. I am just setting off for the library. If anything

should happen to me, Watson will be at the Sandringham B & B in Milton Road, not far from Cambridge station. I'm sorry if this is 'too much information' – but it's very important for me to tell someone what's going on. Have you had any thoughts at all?

Alec

P.S. Sorry. I just meant have you had a chance to think about what I've asked you. I didn't mean, 'Have you had any thoughts *at all?*'

From: Alec
Sent: Saturday 17 January, 11.45pm
To: Wiggy
Subject: Operation Seeward
Attachments: PDF Plan of Library

Dear Wiggy,
Still not having heard from you, I'm afraid I've decided to use you as my confidant anyway. Winterton has been injured, Wiggy. Quite badly. But I'm getting ahead of myself. I should tell the story properly or not at all. This is for the record, isn't it? But oh God, the blood. And the *wounds!*

This evening I entered the library at 5pm, using

my temporary membership. As you will see from the attached plan of the library, the space immediately above the great reading room – accessible by the spiral staircase behind the desk – contains the music stacks, which are not accessible (to readers, anyway) from anywhere else. I had worked out a rather good plan, I thought. The main thing was to distract the dreamy Tawny away from the desk, then sneak up the spiral staircase to the music library, search for the book, and hide there until the library closed at 5.30. Then, using the spare set of master keys that Mary and Tawny have always (rather irresponsibly, in my opinion) left in the top drawer of the enquiries desk, I would let myself out of the reading room, and make my way down Staircase A to the emergency exit next to the cycle racks. Opening the door would set off an alarm, but the idea was that I would quickly hand the book – and the incriminating set of library keys – to Winterton who would be positioned outside. I would then go back inside and face the music with the security man (usually Mike on a Saturday), claiming to have fallen asleep on the floor of the history library before closing time and apologising for causing so much trouble.

Winterton and I would then rendezvous at the nearby Kall-Kwik (just before it closed at 6.30), where we would copy and scan the pamphlet, and I could send the scan straight to you for safe keeping. I brought my laptop along for just that purpose.

I am writing this in A & E. It is 9.45, and I am trying to keep a lid on things! My main concern is for Winterton, of course, but I am also very distracted by the thought that Watson is at the B & B all by himself, and has been on his own since about 4.30pm. What if I'm here all night? But on the other hand, there's no way I can leave. Winterton was delirious by the time we got here. He'd lost so much blood. Pray God he doesn't spill the beans to anyone about exactly how – and why – he got those terrible cuts and gashes. I keep thinking of the bit in *Jane Eyre* when the brother from the West Indies (is it Mason?) is violently attacked in the night, and Rochester forbids him to speak a word of explanation to Jane, as she sits with this unknown bleeding man in the dark, and all the while she can hear the animal-like stirrings of the violent madwoman behind the locked door. This will mean nothing to you if you haven't read the book in question, Wiggy, so I apologise for rambling. It was just that I kept saying pointedly to Winterton in the ambulance, 'Best if you *don't speak*, Winterton, old chap; don't *speak at all*.' And then – just now – I remembered why the situation seemed so familiar, when nothing in my own previous experience has been anything like it.

You will be pleased to hear that the first bit of my plan worked quite well! That's not much consolation to me right now, but I might as well tell the story properly, as I'm probably going to be here for some time. Improvising, I used a cat's miaow to draw Tawny's attention. It's the only animal noise I've ever been able to make; also it seemed appropriate in the circumstances. Anyway, it worked. 'Miaow,' I said. 'Miaaaoooow.' 'Hello?' Tawny said, and left the desk to investigate. As you will see on the plan, there are two sets of swing doors to the reading room (at the same end) so it was quite easy to do the miaow from one side, and then nip round to the other doors and dodge up the spiral staircase while Tawny had gone the other way.

There was no one else up there, thank goodness, but there was one obvious problem to be solved:

I had no idea where Mary had shelved the book! Here were six long walkways of tall stacks, all packed with (mostly) tall, thin musical scores. The Seeward pamphlet, in its protective slipcase, would hardly be conspicuous up here, and I had only twenty minutes to find it before all the lights shut off automatically at 5.30. But I did the right thing. I didn't panic, and I thought about Mary. What would she have done? Where would she hide something in a music library? What did she know about music? Well, not very much. I thought of us watching *University Challenge* together, and Mary cluelessly shouting out the same answer every week – and that was enough. Haydn! She would have hidden it under Haydn!

And so she had. I found the pamphlet tucked behind a score of the Surprise Symphony just before the room was plunged into darkness. It didn't look anything special, I must say, this thin book. It had no aura. When I touched it, there was no responding gust of evil wind, accompanied by the sound of impish whispers from the darker corners of the stack. No, it was just like picking up any book. However, the sheer darkness of the music library after lights out was disconcerting, and I admit I was keen to get out. Luckily, Tawny wasted no time at all in closing up: at 5.31, she could be heard switching off all the desk lamps, humming tunelessly. Then she collected her bag and coat, switched off the main lights, and set the bolt and turned the key to one pair of swing doors; then she set the bolt to the second pair and turned the key from the outside. Only then did I start to creep carefully down the spiral staircase. In the great reading room, the high windows allowed a certain amount of grey light into the room, but it was a while before my eyes grew accustomed to the murk. I coughed, and the sound rang out. I clutched the book in its slipcase to my chest and groped in the drawer for the keys. They weren't there. Why hadn't I brought a torch? I moderated my breathing (I'd started to pant), and continued to feel inside the drawer. And at last I found them. The relief was enormous. But then I heard something – faint and muffled but unmistakeable – that made my blood run cold. A human scream. I now believe that what I heard was Winterton.

Wiggy, I'll have to break off here. They have just told me they are going to keep him in; they've commanded me to go home. They've already given him a transfusion; he is now under sedation; he is definitely on the mend. Well, what a relief! 'Thank you,' I said. I told them I was a mere acquaintance of his, who happened to discover him in his assaulted state – but I also said I knew he had no relatives, so I felt I should wait to see how he was. Everyone has been very kind, although I could have done without them asking, 'Ooh, what's that you're writing?' all the time, and peering at the screen.

It's nearly midnight. It's been a long day, and I'm glad to be leaving. I am desperate to get back to Watson. He is a resourceful little dog – but a little dog none the less.

I just hope Winterton didn't blab much. If he did, they might have put it down to delirium anyway. When they first examined him, they came out and asked if he'd ever been in the navy. I said no, not to my knowledge – for a moment, I imagined they'd found some interesting tattoos. 'It's just that he's been rambling about a captain,' they said. I shrugged. 'Can't explain that,' I said. I have to get back to the B & B. I'll write again as soon as I can.

Alec

From: Wiggy
Sent: Sunday 18 January, 9.41am
To: Alec
Subject: Operation Seeward

Dear Alec,

I have just read your email from late last night, and I don't know what to think. Your stuff is safe with me, of course it is. Send as much as you like. But I feel I ought to tell you that since my breakdown (as everyone calls it) I've been seeing a psychiatrist who has been very helpful – especially with anti-depressants and whatnot – and she warned me that something like this might happen – that I would 'start thinking the Roger stuff was all real again'! Well, I am bloody confused now, I can tell you. You've sent me two bloody audio files of me talking to Roger! And oh my God, he really does sound like Vincent Price!

But all the rest of it – how do I know it's even true? It's like a story. You even keep describing it as a story, Alec, so it's not surprising I'm confused. You could be in Malawi. Or Brighton. You could be tucked up in bed somewhere. You could even be one of the chaps from school. You're not Upton, are you? Bloody Upton; if it is you, I'll bloody kill you. But even if you're really Alec the Quite Unlikely Hero Librarian, you could still be making all this up deliberately. Scheming to drive me mad. They think I didn't lift a finger to find Jo — and in a way I didn't. I noticed those keys to next door were missing; I just didn't think what it meant. And why didn't I? Because I got so absorbed in Roger's story, I forgot I was in one myself.

To be fair, I looked up all the Seeward stuff on the internet, so I know you're not making that up, at least. Actually, I found another bit on YouTube that you probably ought to see — it's a kind of companion piece to the film you watched — I'll send you the link. But I don't want to get sucked in again, Alec. Please don't draw me into this. I'm not strong, like you. In fact, I'm very fragile. This lady-shrink the other day — she brought a fluffy kitten to the consultation room. A kitten. She wanted me to be nice to it.

'Isn't this a bit unorthodox?' I said, but she took no notice. She put the kitten *on my lap.*

I said: 'I don't have a *phobia* about cats, Alison.'

'I know,' she said.

'I'm not scared of them the way people are

scared of spiders — or of their knees suddenly bending the wrong way, and that kind of thing. I just *know how cats think*.'

But she'd made her plan and she was going to stick to it.

'What would you like to say to this lovely little innocent kitten, Wiggy?'

And I looked into its huge eyes and it looked back at me.

'Go on,' she said.

'Go on what?'

'Give it a stroke, Wiggy!' she said.

So I did my best. I made a big effort to stroke its little furry head, but the moment I touched it, it turned round to hiss at me, so I shouted, 'GET OFF MY LAP, YOU BLOODY MURDERING BASTARD, YOU KILLED MY SISTER!'

I'm sorry to hear about Winterton. I do believe you, but I bloody well don't want to. I'd rather think you were Upton in Malawi. I know how lonely you must feel. I have to say your plan sounded very good for a chap who's probably never organised any sort of heist before, and I take my hat off to you. I hope little Watson was well and safe on your return. Of course, I've never met little

Watson myself, and here I am caring about his welfare! What a twerp I'll feel if it turns out he doesn't exist either.

Wiggy

From: Wiggy
Sent: Monday 19 January, 12.32pm
To: Alec
Subject: Hello?

Dear Alec,
You never got back to me yesterday. Could you let me know what's been happening? It's Monday lunchtime. How is Winterton? Wiggy x

From: Wiggy
Sent: Monday 19 January, 5.14pm
To: Alec
Subject: Hello, hello?

Dear Alec,
You're scaring me now, Alec. I've been checking for emails for the last five hours. Just a line would be fine. I just need to know how you and Watson and Winterton are. Wigs x

From: Wiggy
Sent: Monday 19 January, 8.15pm
To: Alec
Subject: Hello

All right. It's evening now, and I've been thinking about things, and perhaps it's my fault you haven't replied all day. Please ignore what I wrote yesterday – all that 'don't know what to think' stuff. All that 'poor me, I'm not well' stuff. I've been reading it back and I can understand if you got cold feet about confiding in me.

I want to help you, Alec, but am I the best person to have on your side? Yes, I've had experience of a talking cat; but think how long I left Jo's phone in the fridge instead of taking it to a phone shop! I was so stupid, Alec. I really thought Roger had taken the phone into the garden to 'play with it'! I had no idea what was going on. I cut out the cryptic crossword for him *every day*, and then helped him fill it in. He would say, 'One down is FAN VAULTING.' And I'd look at the clue, which was 'Jumpy enthusiast often seen in church (3,8)' and I'd say, 'How on earth do you get that?' And he'd drawl, 'It's just a knack, Wiggy. An enthusiast is a fan; jumpy is vaulting. Fan vaulting is often seen in churches.' And I'd say, 'Oh Roger, you're such a brainbox.' And all the time he was demonstrating to me how bloody clever he was, he *knew* Jo was in the cellar next door, and that I could have saved her if I'd known.

So I'm not very clever, and – I have to tell you this, Alec – I'm not very brave. I would never have been as brave as you, creeping around in that library after dark. But it's the Wiggy Brain problem I think you should be wary of most. I was so embarrassed reading my notes about how I imagined Jo and the dog had been taken by aliens. I really did search the area for signs of scorched grass!

Anyway, that's all in the past. I need to know what's happening now. Please let me know. This is torture.

From: Wiggy
Sent: Monday 19 January, 10.36pm
To: Alec
Subject: Alec, where are you?

Alec! For God's sake, I'm going to pieces here. I don't know what to think. Please let me know what has happened. I haven't heard from you for *two days*. I've never met you but *I am your friend*. Wigs

From: Alec
Sent: Tuesday 20 January, 6.03am
To: Wiggy
Subject: None
Attachments: PDF entitled Seeward

Dear Wiggy,
I'm sorry I didn't reply to your emails. I'm sorry if I caused you any distress. The thing is, Winterton is dead. I know. I can't believe it either, but it's true, he's dead. And I don't want to be melodramatic, but I think this might be the last time you hear from me, so I want you to stop being weak about all this because we don't have the luxury. I know no one believes in this stuff, Wiggy. Of course they don't. I wouldn't believe in it either. And I know you've made errors of judgement that make you doubt yourself. But Winterton is dead and Jo is dead, and my own dear Mary is dead – and if I'm next, I have to know that you're not going to delete all this material and take a pill to help you forget it!

Sorry to be harsh. I haven't slept much in the

last seventy-two hours. The only positive thing is that I do have the pamphlet, and I've attached a scan for you to see. Also the dog is safe, thank God. I'm touched that you care about him. But other news is not so good. I had a call on my mobile yesterday morning from someone who said he was Tony Bellingham – his name meant nothing to me but he explained he was that neighbour who called on me after Christmas at home, the one whose surname I'd never taken any interest in. He said there had been a break-in at my house and I needed to go there at once. It was a 'bit of a mess', he said. He was with the police. I said I couldn't go; they demanded to know why not. I said I was at the hospital with a friend who was in a critical condition. I said I would go later, but I shan't. The last thing I want to do is go home. For one thing, he said it was a mess. And it was really neat when I left it, after all that sodding methodical unpacking.

And then, when I got to the hospital, there were police in the ward, and they told me what had happened. In the night, Winterton had died – but nothing to do with his injuries or his blood loss; he died of suffocation, and they were saying it was murder. They said Winterton, under sedation, wouldn't have had much strength to push off his attacker, but the mystery was, how did the attacker get in? I have to tell you, Wiggy: I behaved so *calmly*; I pretended to be concerned but not devastated; shocked, but not alarmed. Much as I wanted to break down on the spot and say, 'I know that evil cats did this! Death and damnation to those evil cats!' I had to pretend that I was as astounded as everyone else that such downright badness existed in the world. So I said pathetic things like 'Why?' and 'Poor fellow' and 'Who would do such a thing?' I let them give me a cup of sweet tea from a machine, and then I hung around, sitting in the corridor, as if too shocked to go home – when all I really wanted was to hang around long enough to find out what had happened.

From what I could piece together, Winterton's room was on the ground floor. A window had been left partly open, but it was much too high off the ground for anyone (other than a large, muscular cat *with powers*, of course) to reach from outside, so they were ruling out anyone climbing in to commit the deed. But it was still murder, the nurse told me. At around 4am, she had been sitting at the nursing station when she heard the alarm from Winterton's heart monitor; she rushed in to find him blue in the face. All over the pillow – and all over Winterton – were weird black hairs, like animal fur. Whoever suffocated Winterton, she said, must have used a black fur jacket or coat to smother him as he slept.

Poor man. How he must have wished – how I wish on his behalf – that on that fateful day on the Acropolis, he had just finished his drawing of fallen masonry, packed up his schoolboy satchel and gone to meet his parents for the long voyage home – without a cat in a basket. But he had read about cats like Roger. '*I've read about cats like you.*' And that was his downfall. I remember Roger saying to you that he suffered for his own hubris on the Acropolis that day; but so did Winterton, in the end.

I haven't had time to read the Seeward pamphlet closely yet, but a lot of it looks so disappointingly lame and predictable – '*All hail Beelzebub, king of cats!*' – that I nearly wept when I first opened it. To think Mary and Winterton died for *this*? Talk about the banality of evil. If Seeward was responsible for writing this – well, I'm sorry to swear, but he must have been a wanker. '*And from out the flames of Hell cometh the Great Cat of All Cats, hail unto the Cat of Cats*' – it goes on and on like that, for pages. But I shan't give up. The main thing that caught my eye was on page seven: the list of Grand Cat Masters, starting with Sir Isaac Newton in 1691. There are about a dozen names altogether, including John Seeward, of course. And as you will see, Seeward names his successor as well, which is very interesting.

I didn't tell you how it went on Saturday night, but I expect you can guess. When I opened the emergency exit at 6pm, I found Winterton on the ground, already bleeding from the neck and head, screaming and thrashing about with a dark shape on top of him. The sound of the klaxon alarm when I opened the door made the Captain shoot off — but I saw him, Wiggy; I saw the Captain's huge yellow eyes watching us in the dark of that dingy courtyard. Mike the security guard appeared with startling speed — in fact, I think my plan of slipping the stolen book to Winterton would never have worked. We'd have been caught in the act. Mike got me to call for the ambulance while he administered first aid. He was so horrified by what had happened — and of course he knew all about the cat that had somehow got into the library on a former occasion — that he couldn't have been less interested in my pathetic rehearsed excuses about falling asleep after tea, stumbling to the wrong door, etc. In a way, the Captain helped me get the pamphlet out of the library, by creating an extremely dramatic diversion.

Wiggy, I'm thinking of moving to a different B & B – it's not only to get away from the landlady's killer air-freshener (although that would be quite sufficient reason, believe me); I just think it's sensible not to stay in any one place for too long. I'll send the address when I can. Would you please study the pamphlet? I must be missing something important. But for the time being, I am going in search of the last Grand Cat Master named on the list, because from what little I can deduce from the mumbo-jumbo all-hail rubbish in *Nine Lives*, he's the key to putting a stop to all this. I'd appreciate it if you would have a look at the last page of the pamphlet, where there is talk of some sort of ritualistic device called a 'Debaser' that the Cat Master 'holdeth' – but what is it? Something about 'a circle closeth'? It makes no sense to me – but as you can imagine, it's hard to think straight right now. It's such a shock to have lost Winterton. And it's irritating, too. Winterton knew so much, Wiggy! Even if he was the most infuriating source of evil-talking-cat information in the world, he was a direct line to Roger – and more importantly, to Roger's history. And now Winterton has been smothered in his hospital bed by – presumably – the Captain lying across his face as he weakly struggled and wriggled and died! I think I know what sort of nightmares my future is full of – assuming I have a future at all.

I can't afford self-pity right now, but I keep thinking that just three weeks ago I was at the seaside, in my lonely cottage, watching Watson run in circles on the beach, indulging myself in my sweetly sad feelings of loss over the sudden and unexplained natural death of Mary. Did I *really* know nothing of all this then? It's impossible to imagine it. I remember how Roger put it to you, when he was telling his life story: that once you've seen the world in a different way, you can't go back. I've had so many new perspectives to deal with in the past couple of weeks that I can hardly keep track of them all. For example, Mary didn't just *die*. Cats are *murdering bastards*. A load of black hairs on a suffocated man's pillow do *not* indicate an assailant using a black fur jacket. The library has been holding powerful cat occult bastard evil *shit* ever since I've worked there. And as for Julian Prideaux – just a few days ago, I was saying that he was the laziest librarian on the planet, and I was mocking the way he used to leave his dandruffy cardigan on the back of his chair! I was wondering how a man of seventy had kept his job when others, like me, had been made to retire at fifty-eight.

And now I know from the list printed in the back of this pamphlet that he is the Grand Cat Master, appointed in person by Beelzebub, and has been so for fifty years, ever since John Seeward hanged himself in the garden at Harville Manor on 3 September 1964.

(By the way, you didn't send that link.)

Telepathic message (also known as an e-miaow)
From: Roger the cat
Sent: Tuesday 20 January, morning
To: Julian Prideaux, Grand Cat Master
Subject: All Hail, Cat Master

All Hail, Cat Master. Roger here. May I approach thy presence, figuratively speaking, oh great librarian and holder of the Great Debaser? From afar, I cringe and fawn unworthily before thy almighty cat power and all-round top-drawer diabolical connections — etcetera, etcetera, etcetera.

E-miaow from Prideaux to Roger
Speak, Roger. This is an unexpected pleasure.

Roger
Yes, I expect it is.

Prideaux
Although I would appreciate it if you tried not to sound so bloody sarcastic. Beelzebub himself ticked me off the other day for not getting the proper respect from you blasted cats. He came all the way from Pandemonium because he found out that the Captain had started calling me 'mate'. I said to him: it's a different world nowadays, Beelzebub. It's not as respectful as it used to be. People on mobile phones; people cycling on the pavement; people cycling across pedestrian crossings even when the lights are against them.

Roger
What did he say to that?

Prideaux
Oh, the usual platitudes. He doesn't care.

Roger
Did he say, 'This is hell, nor am I out of it'?

Prideaux
He did, actually.

Roger
He always says that. He thinks it's funny.

Pause

Roger
I just wanted you to know that I heard.

Prideaux
Heard what?

Roger
About Winterton. About him being polished off in intensive care by 'feline body-surf asphyxiation'.

Prideaux
Roger. Are you upset? I expect you're upset.

Roger
Of course I'm not upset. I'm furious.

Prideaux
Roger, Roger, Roger. If you want to make a formal complaint—

Roger
What, to Beelzebub?

Prideaux
Well, technically, he is our line manager.

Roger
Yes, and I wonder what he'll say when he finds out that, due to your incompetence, a librarian called Alec Charlesworth is now in possession of *Nine Lives* and intends to use it?

Prideaux
What? What did you say?

Roger

He's in possesson of *Nine Lives*.

Prideaux

Alec from periodicals? Look, if this is some sort of joke—

Roger

No joke.

Prideaux

Oh my God, the idea of *Nine Lives* being in the hands of someone like Alec from periodicals! Roger, that book explains everything!

Roger

I know it explains everything, oh Satan's Appointed Deputy. Including how Cat Masters themselves can be destroyed.

Prideaux

Now look. Don't threaten me, Roger. Beelzebub himself—

Roger
Oh, sod Beelzebub.

Prideaux
Roger!

Roger
I'm going to help this periodicals man. He likes Tennyson, and he called his dog after Dr Watson in Sherlock Holmes. He even remembers key passages from *Jane Eyre* in moments of crisis.

Prideaux
Roger, Roger. Stop and think. You're rightly upset about Winterton – but haven't you known for years that the Captain would get to him one day? Isn't it simply a miracle that Winterton managed to elude him for so long? The Captain always blamed Winterton for taking you away from him, all those years ago on the Acropolis. Even when you were both with Seeward after the war, Winterton was in the background, wasn't he? The Captain knew that. When you left the Captain for a second time – when you *chose* to leave him – it really broke his heart.

Roger
He'd already broken mine! No, it's over, oh Great Cat Master. I'm old, I'm jaded. I've even started to look at those people cycling on the pavement and think, 'This *is* hell, nor am I out of it.' I worked it out last night, oh Lord of All Cat Evil: all told, I've been responsible for the deaths of *eight people*.

Pause

Roger
I'm giving you notice. I'm making it nine.

Prideaux
Look. You know you can't kill *me*, Roger. You can't kill the Cat Master! Roger —?

Roger
I can if I read that book.

Prideaux
Roger—!

Roger
All hail, Beelzebub, and all that. See you in hell.

Prideaux
Roger! Roger? Oh, *bugger.*

From: Wiggy
Sent: Tuesday 20 January, 8.45am
To: Alec
Subject: Nine Lives

Dear Alec,
I hope this reaches you. I have been reading this bloody pamphlet for hours now and you're right about how absolutely *wanky* it is – but it's also weirdly plausible, you know. Remember that story you found online about the old man who lived near Harville Manor whose cat came back with a physical aversion to *Songs of Praise*? I can't explain it, but I'm really bloody haunted by that.

Sorry I forgot to send that link to the other bit of footage on YouTube. I'll do it this time. You really ought to see it, Alec. It's dynamite.

I think the best thing about this pamphlet, you know, is the way it implies that *all* cats are basically bastards like Roger deep down, but have gradually lost the ability to practise real evil as the centuries have worn on. Did you pick up on that? The exceptional cats, like Roger and the Captain, aren't the product of some sort of miracle, Seeward says – they just haven't degenerated the way all the others have. I *think* that's what he's saying, anyway. If it is, I think this explains such a lot about cat behaviour, don't you? When they hiss at us, you see, you can tell that they really *expect* us to fall over and die – because that's what used to happen. So when we just stand there, unharmed, and laughing in their faces, they're completely miffed! Huffy, that's cats for you – always got the hump. But why? We've asked ourselves, 'Why are cats so pissed off all the time? They get all the best seats in the house, they have food and warmth and affection. Everything is on their terms, not ours. They come and go as they please. Why aren't they permanently ecstatic?' Well, now it's explained. It's because they're conscious of having lost their ability to do serious evil, and they feel bloody humiliated.

Also, it turns out, the majority of everyday cats feel they've been unfairly abandoned by the Devil! Seeward seems to have taken a sort of cat opinion poll. They *all* still worship him, apparently – but at the same time they know that he doesn't care; that he's too busy cooking up really big evil things like internet banking and double-dip recessions to bother with little furry minions whose only service to him is killing innocent (and insignificant) wildlife. Oh, and that's the other thing! The way they kill birds and mice, and bring them home for us to see! Apparently it's all bollocks about cats bringing us mice and birds because they believe in some childish way that we're their big upright parents who will pat them on the back or something. They do it for only one reason: because birds and mice are their limit, but *they think they'll get their big evil powers back if they only do enough killing.* Anyway, it was fascinating, all of this stuff. Say what you like about Seeward; he really knew his onions about cats. You know the way cats do that trampling thing on your lap, sort of kneading your groin? Well, that's one of these 'vestigial' things as well. It was how cats used to kill people by pretending to be friendly and then severing their femoral arteries! Purring was the way they sent people into a trance, you see — and then, when their prey was sort of paralysed and helpless, the cats would set to work with their claws! That's what all cats are still trying to do, apparently, but not succeeding. I really love an evolutionary explanation for weird things like that, don't you?

Alec, I have to tell you a couple of things and I hope you won't be cross. The first thing showed quite a bit of initiative and pluck, I think. In your last email, you mentioned you were 'going after' the Grand Cat Master, but you weren't everso specific, and I was just reading and re-reading the bit in the book (at the end) about the 'Great Debaser' and it suddenly occurred to me what it was. And I knew you didn't have it, and I thought you'd bloody well want it, if at all possible. I've never explained to you that by sheer coincidence I live just three streets away from the library you used to work in — above the local Kall-Kwik, as it happens. It gave me quite a start when you mentioned the office downstairs as part of your plan for last Saturday night! I never mentioned this before because — well, you didn't ask, Alec, did you? You didn't say, 'And where do you live, Wiggy? Not in Cambridge?' And besides, I wasn't sure at first that I wanted to get involved.

Anyway, I studied the library plan you'd sent me, and this morning I thought I'd bloody well risk it, so I got myself into the library on a rather clever research pretext, and I found Staircase B after getting lost a couple of times, and in the end I found Prideaux's office! I had it all prepared, what I was going to say if I found him in there – how I'd got lost looking for the old 'bindery' office (whatever that is). I thought I might even comment on the awful cardigan. But anyway, he wasn't there, and I got it. Alec, I got the Great Debaser! No idea what to do with it now, of course. But I do have it in front of me as I write this, and I do feel proud.

The other thing I have to tell you isn't quite such a positive-type thing. It's that I've remembered something Roger said to me – as you requested. You may recall that you wrote the other day:

It occurs to me that although the life-story tapes in the folder took him only up to his wartime experiences in the British Museum, he might have told you more — only off the record, as it were.

Well, what I've remembered is that Roger said he knew how to access my emails. Sorry. I know I should have mentioned this before, but it kept flashing into my mind to tell you — especially when you were begging me at the beginning to be your special mate and 'repository' and all that — but then I'd always forget it again.

I'm really sorry, Alec. I mean, I've no idea if Roger *has* been reading every single thing you've sent me. But just in case, my advice would be, *from now on don't tell me anything important by email.* Wx

From: Alec
Sent: Tuesday 20 January, 8.45am
To: Wiggy
Subject: Out of Office Autoreply Re: Nine Lives

I am currently rather busy and mostly away from my computer. If this is Wiggy, I am going to Harville Manor, but don't tell anyone.

From: Wiggy
Sent: Tuesday 20 January, 8.48am
To: Alec
Subject: You should change your autoreply

Alec, You probably ought to change your autoreply. Sorry. See previous email. Wigs x

PART FOUR

Dorset

It has been hard to know where to start with this final instalment of the story. In fact, I have stared at a blank screen for a day and a half, attempting to organise all my impressions of the last act (so to speak) – and simply failing. Perhaps I should wait? Perhaps it's too soon? It was only a week ago that it happened, after all; and it was traumatic, too, by anyone's standards. But if I wait, won't the impressions fade? Won't I forget? And isn't it my duty to get this right? I am beset by questions whose answers are just a matter of opinion. On balance, my feeling is that I should be a man and tackle it now, and put it all behind me. So that's what I will do. I will have another cup of tea, and then I'll pull myself together (and try not to repeat the unfortunate expression 'be a man', which I've never used before in my life) and press on and just pray that I remember to put everything in.

To get me started, I thought it would be helpful to establish a few basic things about the outcome; to set the guidelines, as it were. I have answered the multiple choice questions below with absolute honesty, which has not been easy. As you will see, there are some aspects of the story that I can't yet quite confront – see my answer to question 3, in particular. But question 2 was by far the hardest for me, and I may yet cave in and change my answer from the pathetic 'Not entirely' to 'Yes, I feel terrible'. Because, was it all my own fault? Take Watson. It was certainly my fault that this innocent creature – a friend to all the world, and the bravest of souls – accompanied me to Harville. It was my fault, also, that Dr Winterton put himself in the Captain's way outside the library on that fateful Saturday evening; likewise, Wiggy would hardly have turned up when he did, if I hadn't absolutely insisted on his getting involved in my investigations. However, as much as I want to take the blame for everything, I do remind myself that, when you boil it down, Beelzebub and all his demonic feline deputies (from the seventeenth century onwards) are much, much more culpable in all this than I could ever be.

Anyway, here are the questions.

1. Did things turn out well, generally speaking, Alec?
Yes, very well ☐   No ☐   Not really ☑   Don't ask ☐

2. If NO, was it your own fault? (Think carefully.)
Yes, I feel terrible ☐   No ☐   Not entirely ☑   Don't ask ☐

3. Was anyone hurt?
Yes ☐   No ☐   Not really ☐   Don't ask ☑

4. Has the world been rid of the evil cats?
Miraculously, yes ☑   Worryingly, no ☐   Too early to tell ☐

5. How do you feel about cats now?
Love them ☐   Indifferent ☐   Conflicted ☑   Hate them ☐

6. How do you feel, facing the future?
Happy ☐   Relieved ☐   Numb ☑   Don't ask ☐

7. Would you consider a holiday in Dorset in the near future?
Yes ☐ No ☐ Not on your life ☑

So, I went to Harville Manor. I set off shortly after sending my last email to Wiggy – which I find, looking back, was timed at 6.03am on the Tuesday after Winterton was murdered. In retrospect, I now think I should have waited to make a proper plan. I should also have tried to get some sleep. But I was angry and agitated and I couldn't go home, and I *loathed* the smell of that bloody air-freshener, I can't emphasise enough how disgusting it was, and I also felt compelled to do something. So I strapped Watson into his car-seat harness, de-iced the windscreen as well as I could, turned up the heater and set my satnav for Dorset. It was a freezing, frosty morning in Cambridge, and heavy snow was predicted for the whole of the south of England before nightfall – but such a cheerless forecast did not deter me; quite the reverse. It made me all the more eager to get started. My satnav predicted a journey of under four hours (arrival time 10.02am), but I sensibly took this information with a pinch of salt. Satnavs are always making precise – but totally irresponsible – prognostications of that sort. The main things were to arrive in daylight and beat the snow. My plan, as I set off, was to stop for breakfast once I was safely south-west of London. And then, having steadied myself with a bit of necessary nutritional ballast (I hadn't eaten a proper meal since before the library adventure the previous Saturday), I would seriously – *at last* – study the Seeward pamphlet. I had every confidence that, with the priceless information I found there, I would find a way – *at last* – to put an end to the big black devil-cat that, first of all, had terrified my wife at the library by ripping a small inoffensive study room to splinters, and then had come to our house and felled her in the garden with a single satanic hiss.

Watson went to sleep on the passenger seat. Looking at him snoozing peacefully beside me, I wondered whether he had remembered to bring his old service revolver. To wake him up just to ask him, however, would be taking the joke too far – even though this was the one and only occasion in our lives when it would be appropriate to say the line. The *Today* programme held my attention for about ten minutes – but then I had to switch it off. News from the real world, concerning such burning topics as budget deficits and Syria, seemed just bizarre to me in both its scale and its irrelevance. I realised it had been a long time since I'd cared a bean about any other topic than the evil that cats do. Given my previous character, this development was quite remarkable. Whoever would have thought that a chap like me – who took the *Guardian* daily; who had never missed a *Newsnight* unless deeply indisposed or out of the country; and who sent funny letters to *Private Eye* (which they sometimes printed) – could turn so completely metaphysical overnight? But so it was. In fact, it seemed to me that every single item on the news – concerning economic doom and political hypocrisy and social breakdown – was not 'news' at all. What I could hear was just a series of utterly transparent ploys to frighten and alarm the listeners – and frighten them, moreover, about the wrong things.

The snow started to fall just after I'd skirted London; the added urgency made me decide – rather stupidly – not to stop for breakfast after all. It was a day, I must confess, in which I made countless errors of judgement. Deciding not to eat anything, when I was already phenomenally

light-headed, was arguably at the root of many of
my subsequent mistakes. Of necessity, I did make
a stop for fuel (and the lavatory) at a bright Esso
petrol station, where I gave Watson a quick chance
to stretch his legs and sniff some filthy roadside
grass, but otherwise I considered it best to keep
going. Drive now, eat later — this was my over-
confident scheme. The snow fell more heavily as I
crossed the county border into Dorset — on either
side of the road, fields and roofs and driveways
were turning to a solid white, but the roads
remained passable while it was daylight and I drove
on steadily, with my old-fashioned windscreen
wipers noisily knocking the snow to the edges of
the glass, and the view ahead (in the headlights)
made vertiginous by streams of atoms all apparently
rushing to collide with the car. Formerly, on such
mentally exhausting drives as this, Mary and I
would have taken turns at the wheel. But now I was
alone, and travelling at 15 miles per hour, and I
kept myself amused just by checking the way the
satnav airily adjusted my predicted time of arrival
(10.53am! 11.27am! 1.32pm! 2.07pm!) — with
never an apology or acknowledgement, of course,
for having been so absurdly optimistic up to now.

A hundred yards short of the gateway to Harville Manor (*'In one hundred yards you will reach your destination'*), I stopped the car in a lay-by under a street lamp next to an ancient wall, switched off both the engine and the windscreen wipers, and allowed the snow to settle, slowly and silently, on the glass. I needed to think. Something Wiggy had written had nagged at me while I drove — that he was now aghast to realise that having been so caught up in Roger's story, he had neglected to look for Jo. Had I let something similar happen to me? Had I forgotten to grieve for Mary? Of course, both Wiggy and I could argue that the cat story concerned us personally — but I had to face facts. When Tony whatsit from next door had told me about Winterton looking for me (when I first returned from the coast), it had made me happy. I had felt excited; I had been thrilled that I was going to learn more; I was so agog to 'fill in the gaps'. And at that point, I had no idea that Mary's death had any connection to Roger, or the Captain, or even to Winterton himself. It was all right to argue that my eager and obsessive pursuit of this story had been about avenging Mary: there was some truth in that. But at the same time I needed to admit that pursuing these evil cats had also been a very effective way of putting her dreadful loss right out of my mind.

Sitting here now, inside this rapidly cooling vehicle that Mary and I had purchased together eight years before, I felt desolate, stupid, tired, a bit cold and (above all) weak with hunger. With a sort of morose satisfaction, I watched as the falling snow silently and inexorably coated the windscreen, effectively sealing Watson and me from the view beyond. When there was no view left at all — when a weird yellow darkness filled the car — I allowed myself first to close my eyes; and then I allowed myself to cry.

Naturally, Watson bore the brunt again. 'Watson, I'm sorry,' I said. What had I done? Why were we here? I had driven halfway across the country, in a heavy snowfall, possibly putting myself and the dog at unnecessary risk — and all because of a story that needed an ending. As if stories ever did end anyway.

I undid Watson's harness and pulled him on to my lap — and he licked the tears from my face, the ways dogs always do, because they like the taste. I thanked him and smiled, and started to pull myself together. 'Watson,' I said, with a sigh. 'If this isn't all classic displacement activity, I'd like to know what is.'

And then we both heard and felt it together – something softly landing on the roof of the car. Watson barked, and I told him to shush. If I had been sensible, I'd have started the engine and used the windscreen wipers – and driven off smartly, as well. But it wasn't as simple as that; for one thing, I couldn't bear to disturb our feeble, snowy cocoon. Also, it wasn't just that I didn't want to see what was out there: I absolutely didn't want *it* to see *me*.

'Perhaps it will go away,' I whispered to Watson.

But from the roof of the car, it jumped down and landed on the bonnet – the car bouncing a little, but not enough (thank goodness) to shift the snow on the windscreen. Paralysed, with one hand on the ignition key and the other across Watson's shoulders, I could make out the merest dark shape beyond the layers of glass and snow – moving from side to side, as if sniffing at the snow, less than fifteen inches from my face. Watson growled, and I couldn't blame him. I felt like growling myself. Ten seconds must have passed like this, and then another ten. And then, just as I was withdrawing my hand from Watson, to take the steering wheel, and whispering, 'It'll be all right,' an enormous cat's paw struck violently at the windscreen, and we both jumped in the air. The first strike was followed by a rapid volley of blows — *Bam! Bam! Bam, bam, bam!* — that shattered the caked snow and sent it flying in shards — and revealed the terrifying sight of the Captain on the Volvo's bonnet, huge and black and yowling, and at extremely close range.

'Get off my car!' I shouted (I wish I could say I thought of something better than that, but I didn't).

'Wuff, wuff, wuff! Wuff, wuff, wuff, wuff!' said Watson.

'Get off, get off!' I repeated.

'Wuff, wuff, wuff!' repeated Watson.

I started the engine and the windscreen wipers. Undeterred, the cat continued to beat at the glass, his claws making bright white dents and pits. What were those claws *made of*, for goodness' sake? And what could I do? I couldn't help remembering the mess he'd made of that carrel in the library. What if the next thing he tore to pieces and left a claw stuck in (by way of gory calling-card) was *me*? My only option was to put the car in gear and gingerly move off. Surely the Captain would jump clear once we were in motion? But he didn't. In fact, he seemed to think nothing of balancing on the snowy, slippery bonnet of a slow-moving Volvo driven without much conviction by a recently retired periodicals librarian who hadn't had a proper meal for days.

'Get off my car!' I yelled again.

But he clung on easily, and kept chopping and bashing at the windscreen, which was – oh God! – beginning to crack and fracture. Again, I blame my foolish decision to pass up the chance of a quick sausage sandwich at a Little Chef; it might have made all the difference. Because, contrary to my normal Hamlet-y disposition, I failed to think things through. Rightly it occurred to me that braking to throw the Captain off was out of the question because Watson was unharnessed and might be hurt. But beyond that, I just couldn't think, so I did a ridiculous thing: I accelerated. On the slippery road, I revved the engine and drove fast towards the gateway to Harville Manor, all the while shouting at the cat (absurdly) to *get off the car*; and then made an abrupt turn, hoping the Captain would be thrown clear by the sudden change in direction. But I lost control of the turn. And when the car slid to the right (as it was bound to), it hit the right-hand gatepost broadside with considerable momentum. 'Watson!' I said. The bang as we hit the post was terrific. The Captain shot off and hit a brick wall. The back door on my side caved in, and poor Watson was thrown sideways against the passenger door (and I have to admit, he screamed).

The good thing was, when the dust settled, the Captain had disappeared from view. The bad thing was, I had probably now written off the car, and the snow was falling more heavily than ever.

But the engine was miraculously still running, so I risked attempting to drive off. With a scrunch and rasp of metal, I edged the Volvo forward, unable to make out anything much about the way ahead – what with the snow and the damaged wipers and the buggered glass. Where was the Captain? There was no sign. Had he run off? Was he lying in front of the car? Was he possibly . . . dead? Well, I will never forget the strange satisfaction of feeling the car mount a tell-tale bump on the road, and drop down again. 'Oops,'

I said aloud. I couldn't be sure it was him, because I couldn't see. But if that was the Captain being run over by my battered car – well, hooray. Halfway up the drive, I stopped and gave Watson a reassuring hug – but it was more for my own reassurance than for his. Had the dear dog been hurt? He had hit the door with force, but he appeared to be all in one piece – and, for the first time since we had set out that day, I saw his tail wag a little, as if he were enjoying himself. One never knows how much of a situation a dog is taking in. I mean, I couldn't swear to it, because I was a bit traumatised – but I *think*, when we ran over the Captain (or possibly it was when I quickly reversed and drove over the bump for a second time, just to be sure), I heard a Daniel Craig voice beside me make the laconic remark, 'Nice one.'

I need hardly say that running over the Captain had not been part of my plan. But let's face it, I had no plan. So if the Captain was dead, did it matter that it wasn't a big dramatic end – involving crucifixes and exposure to daylight and a stake through the heart? As I carried on driving at a snail's pace towards the house – the car hardly gripping at all on the snowy driveway – I was reminded of something Mary's father used to say about playing golf, when he'd shot a quite poor round technically but had nevertheless emerged with a decent score. 'There are no pictures on the scorecard, Alec!' Well, I suddenly saw the truth of this peculiar statement of the obvious – because, narratively satisfying or not, the score at present was:

Alec I   Cats 0

– and that was surely good enough, even if the Great Cat of Cat Evil had just been vanquished, sort of unintentionally, under the wheels of a classic Swedish saloon car of legendarily robust construction.

But I soon forgot the Captain in any case, because, arriving at the house, I had my first sight of Roger. Yes, Roger was here! And when I spotted him – sitting high up on one of those curly-wurly Elizabethan chimneys, solemnly swinging his grey tabby tail and watching us proceed up the drive – I'm ashamed to say my heart leapt. Despite his proven wickedness, there was something in Roger that simply captivated me. How unlike the

Captain he was in every regard! Of course, I shouldn't forget that the two cats had a lot in common. Both Roger and the Captain were Nine Lifers – with all the concomitant Nietzschean overtones. They had both travelled romantically through the remains of ancient civilisations, often by moonlight, reading and reciting poetry; they had hobnobbed with the Durrells; most impressive of all, they had mastered the complexity of Greek ferry timetables. According to the photograph in the 'Roger' file, they had also both lazed happily in the grass beneath the swinging corpse of a man who had been their nominal Master in this world. But now they were poles apart. Whereas the Captain seemed to represent only the worst things in cats (murderous instinct, territorial violence, shattering toughened windscreens with bare claws), Roger stood for all that was best – elegance, beauty, fine whiskers and supreme intellectual poise.

I got out of the car and sank an inch or two into the thick snow.

'Roger?' I called. With three or four neat bounding motions, Roger descended to the ground to meet me. It was like a dream.

'Alec,' he said.

He knew me. How on earth did he know me? I didn't care. He held out a paw; I bent down and shook it. His eyes were so green. No one had mentioned before the sheer beauty of Roger's piercing green eyes.

'Welcome to hell,' he said, and laughed. I laughed too. Good grief, I couldn't believe it. It was the Vincent Price voice – in person!

'We ought to get inside. We don't have long to get organised. Did you bring the dog?'

I said yes, I had brought him. Again, how did he know about the dog? What was it that needed to get organised? From inside the car, Watson barked.

'Ah, Watson,' said Roger. 'Come at once if convenient. If inconvenient, come all the same.'

Five minutes later, we were inside the manor, which was no improvement, temperature-wise; it was considerably colder, in fact. Stamping my feet, I stood at a leaded window overlooking the darkening orchards while Roger sat on the wooden sill and indicated features of interest near to the house. Watson I had tied up in a far corner, and he had

finally stopped barking — which was a relief, because
everything echoed spookily in this shell of a house.
To whom did Harville Manor now belong, I
wondered. To Prideaux? Was this where he had
always been when his cardigan was so artfully hung
on the back of that chair in Special Collections,
and the rest of us had covered for him? If so, he
certainly hadn't bothered to make it comfortable
for himself here. No power was switched on; a
few old office chairs had been herded into a dark
corner; a few stubs of candles had been left around
on the naked oak floorboards. Any vague and
far-fetched hopes I might have entertained concerning
a nice welcome-to-Dorset afternoon tea in front
of a big manorial log fire were now in ruins. To
someone who had insanely passed up his every
chance for an infusion of sausage sandwich on the
road, this was very hard.

'There's the old well over there,' said Roger. I
looked, obediently. My stomach made a little
growling noise.

'There's a story attached to it, of course, about
witches, but it takes forty-eight minutes so I shan't
start.'

I laughed. 'That's a shame,' I said.

'I know, but there you are. There's the tree where Seeward hanged himself. I expect you want to know all about Seeward?'

'Yes, please. I'll get a chair.'

'Oh, but that would take at least an hour.'

I located a chair and pulled it over to the window. I needed not to be standing.

'There,' I said, with a puff as I sat down. 'It was a long drive.'

'Of course, yes,' said Roger, understandingly. 'And what time did you run over the Captain?'

He said it as if he were enquiring what time I'd come through Dorchester.

'I'm sorry?' I said. 'What time did I do *what*?'

'You ran him over, Alec. It's OK. I just need to know roughly when you did it.'

'Well, it was just now.'

'Good. So we've got about an hour before he comes back.'

'You mean—?'

'Of course.'

'He'll come back?'

'Of course he will. That's why we're here, Alec.'

'Right, yes.'

Deep down, I had known this. But it was sad

to see that my scorecard was as undependable as the satnav. It had just reverted to:

Alec 0   Cats 0

'Pay attention, Alec,' said Roger. 'This is no time for one of your mental digressions. The Captain must be stopped, and the book you stole will help us. Seeward wrote it all down, you see. How to dispose of Nine Life cats – and their master – for good and all. That's why Seeward left instructions for it to be burned. That's why the Captain has been so desperate to get it back. Now, there are two stages to defeating the Captain, the method for both of which is specified in Seeward's book—'

I interrupted him. I couldn't help it. I was nearly in tears. Someone was actually telling me something! 'Roger,' I gushed, 'thank you, thank you for telling me all this.'

'You're welcome. But—'

'It's been really hard!'

'Yes, I'm sorry. It must have been.'

'So thank you. That's all I wanted to say. Thank you.'

'Right.'

'That's all. Sorry.'

'That's fine. Now where was I?'

'You were saying there were two stages to destroying the Captain.'

'Oh yes. The point is, we must deprive him of both his powers and his immortality. The first requires us to employ the Great Debaser – which we might not have access to. But the second is by far the more important in any case.'

'Roger?' I said.

'Yes?'

I hesitated. I wanted to say that I loved the way he had said 'more important' rather than 'most important' in that sentence. But perhaps it would be inappropriate to comment on matters of correct English at such a critical moment, so I just said, 'Nothing. Go on.'

'I happen to know,' he said, 'that all Nine Lifers lose their immortality if the Great Cat Master is killed by one of his own cat minions.'

'Yes?'

Roger took a deep breath and then said quietly, 'I have vowed to kill Prideaux and I will do it this day.'

My mind raced. This was quite a big development.

Didn't it mean that now Roger would be mortal himself?

I didn't know what to say. What I *wanted* to say was, 'Roger, I can't even remember why I'm here any more; I'm losing my grip.' Instead, I said weakly, 'Roger, have you got a plan, then? I thought I had a plan, but you know what it's like when you wake up from a dream and the plan isn't a plan after all; it turns to water in your brain? It's like that! But it sounds like you've got a good one. Have you? Have you got a plan?'

He laughed.

'You know about Prideaux?' he said, jumping down from the windowsill. 'Of course you don't know *everything* about Prideaux, but if I told you *everything* about him it would take a hundred and six minutes and that's no good because he'll be here in half an hour. My plan concerns Prideaux first, and then the Captain, and then . . . me.'

He paused. It was fascinating to watch his great cat-brain at work. I felt totally useless – and it must have showed, because Roger was evidently aware of the need to console me.

'Your running over the Captain gives my plan much more chance of success, though, Alec.'

'Really?'

'Yes. And actually, by the time Prideaux gets here, the snow on top of the Captain's body will be quite deep, so with any luck Prideaux will run him over again, giving us yet another hour of breathing space.'

This seemed a little cold-hearted. However, I was hardly in a position to judge, given my callous reversing-over-the-body-and-running-over-it-again thing from earlier.

'So first, I need to see the pamphlet for myself,' said Roger. 'You did bring it?'

I went to the car and retrieved Seeward's pamphlet from the back seat. I did this with a certain feeling of defeat. People had died on account of *Nine Lives*. I myself had stolen it from a library. The fact that I'd gained virtually no enlightenment from it made me feel unbelievably stupid.

'I'll gladly give you this,' I said, when I returned indoors, 'if you'll fill in the gaps for me, Roger. You do know everything, don't you?'

'Yes,' said Roger. 'Yes, I do.'

I handed over the pamphlet. Expertly, he turned the pages with his claws, and found what he was looking for.

'Good. I just needed to see this in hard print,' he said. 'You never know with a PDF . . .'

Watching him read — watching those beautiful green eyes devour the information on the page — I was quite overcome. I had never admired anyone so much in my life.

'Ah,' he said at last. 'It really is as simple as that!' He held up a paw and flexed his claws. He purred with happiness. God, he was beautiful.

'What does it say?'

'I'd like to tell you, but it would take — hang on.' He made a mental calculation. 'It would take three days.'

'You keep saying things like that, Roger. I wish you'd stop saying that there isn't time to tell me things! I have to know more. That's why I stole that thing and drove down here.'

I sounded peevish, but I was too exhausted to correct my tone. 'Why did Jo have to die in that cellar?' I demanded, and started using my fingers to indicate where I was on a long list of points. 'Why didn't you tell Wiggy where she was? What did the Captain do to Mary? What happened to you after the war years in the British Museum? What did Wiggy find on YouTube that I didn't?

Why did you fall out with the Captain, when you'd
been such very close friends? Why has the Captain
turned out this way?'

Roger seemed surprised by the intensity of my
questioning.

'Winterton didn't tell you anything?'

I made a 'Ha!' noise. 'He was hopeless! Winterton
started every story in the middle. It drove me mad.'

Roger sighed.

'Look, Alec. I've got time to tell you this much.
What happened at Shingle Cottage was this.
Prideaux tracked me down.'

'He's your master?'

'He's my master. I've eluded him for decades,
but in the end he always tracks me down. The
Captain helps him. It's been the same pattern over
and over: I find a human I want to live with quietly;
I start to tell my story, which is fairly lengthy—'

'I know.'

'—and I am always stopped by Prideaux, one
way or another, before I can tell anyone the terrible
truth of what happened here at Harville.'

'What did happen here?'

'Oh, Alec,' Roger said, with a catch in his voice.
'You don't want to know. All I can say is that it

sometimes involved' — and here he found it hard to speak — 'it involved kittens.'

As he said the word 'kittens', he closed his beautiful eyes and a great shiver of horror rippled right through him, from the end of his handsome tail right up to the top of his head.

'Seeward was a monster,' he went on. 'Prideaux worshipped him. He has given his life to preventing the truth of Seeward's experiments from getting out. This time, having traced me to Shingle Cottage, he planned to snatch me away — and my biggest regret now is that I didn't just co-operate. But it got complicated. Jo spotted Prideaux prowling about.'

'The binoculars?'

'Exactly. She made notes of dates and times. And then she started seeing that big cat as well, she got frightened, and I felt I couldn't leave her.'

'And then you killed that poor little dog.'

'Of course I didn't kill the dog!'

I bit my lip. 'I'm sorry, I thought you did.'

'Well, I didn't. Oh Alec, I loved that dog. Prideaux killed the dog because it was protecting me. When Jo found poor Jeremy dead, she got hysterical, and that's when I suggested she hide in the cellar next door. I thought it was quite a clever idea; I knew she had those keys; I thought she would be safe. Jo loved me, Alec. You've seen the photograph of her holding me; you know she painted wonderful portraits of me. Didn't she phone Wiggy to say, "Help me take care of Roger!" on the day it all happened? She begged me to hide with her, you know. But I was afraid it would make things worse for her if I did.

'My mistake was to scarper. It was only after I was sure Prideaux had gone that I came back to the cottage and realised Jo was missing. I tried to get into the house next door but it had been locked up. From the windowsill, I could see into the kitchen — and I could see that a heavy trunk had been placed over the cellar trapdoor, making it impossible for Jo to get out. This was typical of Prideaux's sadism: if he couldn't catch me, he could teach me a lesson — *This is what happens to people if you try to tell your story, Roger.* He knew what it would be like for me, enduring Jo's slow death, knowing it was all my fault and powerless to help. I don't ask for your sympathy, Alec. I know I don't merit it. But don't forget, I am the one person you will ever meet who knows from their own experience what it's like to die like that, slowly and horribly, in a vile, airless hole.

'It was three days before Wiggy arrived. And I know what you're going to ask, and I want to set something absolutely straight. You keep asking, "Why didn't Roger tell Wiggy where Jo was? Why didn't Roger *say*?" Well, you're forgetting something, Alec. You've got quite accustomed to a crucial idea that a month ago you would have dismissed as utterly preposterous. How long do you think it takes for me to break the news to each new person that I am a talking cat? Well, check back in your precious files. It was several days before I said those first clear words to Wiggy, "Let me out" – and if you recall, he was freaked out by them and refused to believe his ears. By the time I could talk to Wiggy properly, the scratching noises had long since ceased. By the time he was writing James Bond scenes for me, my lovely brave Jo was most definitely dead.'

It would take a while for me to process all this. In the meantime I had just one question.

'So why did you pee on the phone when it was charging?'

'To destroy that terrible picture of the dog.

Prideaux took the picture and replaced the phone on its charger. Alec, can you imagine how dangerous it is to pee directly on to a phone that's charging at the mains? If any more proof were needed that I cared about Jo and couldn't bear what had happened to her, it's that I risked *electrocution of the penis* to destroy that terrible thing.'

Half an hour later, as darkness finally engulfed the house, we were aware of a car on the drive. We both strained to hear whether Prideaux would run over the Captain, and were relieved to hear the unmistakeable ker-bump from the drive that meant we'd been let off getting swiped at by gigantic beastly claws for at least another sixty minutes or so. I even let out a small cheer ('Yay!'), which was heartless of me, but also fairly understandable in the circumstances. Roger was worried that Prideaux would guess the cause of the bump, and maybe stop to dig the Captain's body out of the snow — but there were no sounds of car doors, or shovels, or indeed cries of horror, and in due course Prideaux arrived at the house.

He was older than I'd remembered him. He stood up straighter. But when was the last time I had seen him? Casting my mind back, it was probably the retirement party for old Hopkins in the classification department. Hoppy (as we affectionately called him) had made a dreadfully ill-considered speech about how — if asked — he would set about classifying some of his colleagues according to the laborious 'Beacham' university system, and it had been an unmitigated disaster, offending everyone present. Prideaux had walked out! Poor Hoppy had died within a few months of retirement, of course. As I now recalled (with a familiar sinking feeling), it was said that Hoppy's newly adopted cat had tragically tripped him at the top of the stairs.

'Charlesworth! Unbelievable!' huffed Prideaux, as he entered. He was evidently not at all pleased to see me here. Roger and I were sitting on a pair of the office chairs, in a patch of moonlight from one of the leaded windows. Roger had arranged the furniture for Prideaux's arrival in a sort of circle. I had lit a few of the old wax candle stubs. Basically, it looked (ho hum) like the setting for the inevitable seance.

'Why on earth are you here, Charlesworth?' he went on. 'This is between me and the cats. Nothing to do with you. So *piss off!*'

Now, before I proceed with this account, I feel I have to make something very clear. It's true that I was sensationally light-headed by this point. It's true that I was weak and hysterical due to a fundamental lack of sausage sandwich. I had crashed the car. I had fallen in love with a pair of green eyes. I had thrown an infantile tantrum when a cat called Roger wouldn't tell me immediately everything I wanted to know. And now I was reeling with all the new knowledge that Roger had helpfully supplied. Nevertheless, I stand by everything that happened at Harville, however far-fetched, and I am telling you that when Prideaux turned his face to me and said 'Piss off!', his eyes *went red*. I don't mean they went a little bit red-rimmed like Kenneth Branagh's when he's being Wallander on the telly. When Prideaux said 'Piss off!' to me, his whole eyeballs were not only bright red but *illuminated*, like traffic lights.

I was so startled that I giggled. This man can't have satanic eyeballs, I thought. He's a librarian.

'Where's the Captain?' he snapped. 'And what's that dog doing in here? Seeward would turn in his grave! And as for you—' He pointed to Roger. 'Have some damned respect!'

Roger jumped down from his office chair, and looked up at Prideaux. 'Hail, oh Cat Master,' he said.

I giggled again. I don't know why I couldn't take it seriously; I just couldn't.

'That's more like it,' said Prideaux. 'Roger, come here. Approach.'

Roger turned his back on Prideaux, and then did something I didn't imagine a cat could do. With all four legs bent obsequiously low, he crawled slowly backwards towards Prideaux (it was something like moonwalking), and sat himself demurely at his master's feet.

Prideaux reached down and stroked Roger's ears as a reward. Roger narrowed his beautiful green eyes, thrashed his tail a couple of times, and then (apparently) submitted.

To my own surprise, I piped up, 'Can we have a light on?'

'Where's the Captain?' Prideaux demanded again (ignoring me). 'He said he'd be here before me.'

'He was detained, oh Great Cat Protector and Servant of Beelzebub,' said Roger. 'But he isn't far.'

'That's true,' I said, and pulled a face. I wasn't drunk, I swear it. But I couldn't seem to control myself. Those flashing red eyes had been more than I could take.

Prideaux turned to me. 'You have two things that belong to me, Charlesworth,' he said. His voice went big and echoey and the traffic-light eyes came back. I burst out laughing again. Honestly, it was *hilarious*.

'Two?' I squeaked.

'Seeward's book and the Great Debaser. And I want them *now!*'

This time, when he flashed his red eyes at me, a spark of flame flew out and set fire to the floorboards.

'Oh my God, be careful!' I said, stamping out the spark. And then everything went swimmy, and I found I was gazing at Roger, sitting so demurely at Prideaux's feet – his green eyes glowing almost as much as Prideaux's red ones.

'He hasn't eaten for *days*, oh Cat Master,' said Roger. 'He's not important. He knows nothing.'

'Huh,' said Prideaux.

I tried to say something but my mouth wouldn't move, and I fell sideways off the chair. I had always said I'd been captivated by Roger, but previously I had meant it metaphorically.

* * *

Obviously, I'm sorry I missed a whole chunk of the proceedings of that big night at Harville. Just when things started getting truly interesting, I lapsed into a coma! Looking back, I can't help wondering: was it Roger's doing, or was I simply very tired? Either way, it's safe to say that when I woke up, things had radically moved on. From somewhere Prideaux had found a sort of wooden throne, and was now seated on it with Roger on his lap, and he was making an incantation. I was still lying on the floor where I'd fallen, next to the office chair. I wondered, should I let anyone know that I'd returned to the land of the living? Would it be wise to put my hand up and ask if we could watch the telly? I glanced at Roger, and he shook his head at me, so I stayed where I was. And that's how I witnessed it all — a bit like Watson playing dead for the sake of a biscuit, I was playing dead in order to see all this: the candle flames leaping up, gold and red, to the ceiling; the doors and windows pulsating to a mighty wind; red sulphurous smoke rising from the floorboards. Although I had never personally been in such a situation before, it was clear to me that someone was coming, someone was definitely *coming* — and it wasn't, probably, the man from the fourth emergency service.

But at the same time, this ritual of summoning the Devil clearly wasn't going to plan for Prideaux. On his lap, Roger was purring, and Prideaux was saying, 'Not now, Roger! Not now.' He tried to knock Roger off, but the cat clung on, and purred more loudly – menacingly loudly. His purr, in fact, grew so loud and deep and resonant that I could feel the vibration in the floor, and Prideaux's throne was shaking. Watson, in his corner, started to bark. Meanwhile the smoke was still rising, and the wind still howling round the house, but Prideaux was no longer chanting – he had stopped abruptly, as if silenced by a greater power.

The purr grew louder still, and louder, and then Prideaux screamed. As I watched him, Roger started to make an exaggerated puddling motion in his Master's lap. And suddenly a geyser of scarlet blood shot high into the air.

'Aaaaah!' screamed Prideaux, as Roger's claws dug deep into his groin. More blood spurted; Roger ignored it. He kept purring and he kept puddling, his shoulders working up and down, as his claws pierced and ripped Prideaux's flesh, tearing his life away.

At this point a large, dark figure began to

materialise in the middle of the candle flames – a figure with unmistakeable goatish overtones.

'Master!' screamed Prideaux. 'Master, stop him!'

But Roger wasn't to be swayed from his grisly task. His claws dug deeper and deeper. Blood was now spurting in all directions, and the almighty purr was deafening.

'Get off me!' Prideaux screamed (without result) as his blood rained down on Roger, on the chairs, on everything. Meanwhile the figure continued to materialise within the circle; it began to look about it; it began to emit a smoky glow. And then—

Bang!

A great knock at the door echoed through the room, and the figure looked round in confusion. Watson, whose barking had got ever more hysterical in his corner, broke free and hurled himself towards the door.

Bang! Bang!

More knocking. The figure noticed me lying on the floor just as Watson turned round and (oh no) noticed him. It was the worst moment of all, as far as I was concerned: to see my brave little dog charging at the satanic figure, barking and growling; skidding and sliding on Prideaux's blood. 'No, Watson, no!' I shouted. 'Stop it, Watson! Stop that!'

Bang! Bang! Bang!

And then it all happened very quickly. Just as the figure turned to deal with Watson, Roger leapt from Prideaux's lap on to the floor, smothered in blood, and confronted the apparition.

'Beelzebub,' he said in a commanding voice. Their eyes met. 'Your servant is dying. Look.'

It was true. Prideaux had stopped screaming and his breathing was shallow. His blood had stopped spurting. His life was seeping from him on his throne. The apparition became instantly unsteady. It began to fade, dip, swirl and hum. The force was like a helicopter out of control, spinning to its destruction.

Bang! Bang!

The renewed knocking startled us all, as did the big door opening. As we turned to see who it was, the figure vanished, turning inside out, as if disappearing into a black hole. At the very last breath of Prideaux and the very last tiny wisp of the apparition, a man appeared at the door, and Watson — who never gives up, really — ran off to bark at him, the way he barks at everyone.

'Who is it?' demanded Roger. 'Who's there?'

And thus Wiggy entered, with perfect dramatic timing – to find me prone on the floor, the Devil disappearing, Watson hysterical, Prideaux a corpse and Roger caked head to tail in bright red arterial blood.

But his arrival was not the end of it all, because Wiggy had not come alone. We had scarcely time to get our breath back before 'Is this the Captain?' Wiggy said, indicating a large black bundle in his arms. 'Can you believe it, I found him in the road! Bloody hell, I nearly ran him over!'

There was no time for introductions – or indeed for explanations. I made a valiant effort and got up off the floor, just as the Captain leapt from Wiggy's arms and approached Roger on menacing tiptoe, his back hunched high, his tail swishing.

'Hello,' I said quickly to Wiggy.

'Hello,' he whispered back.

Roger stood his ground, but it would have been clear to anyone: he was no match for the Captain in any conventional cat fight.

'What have you done here, Roger?' the Captain demanded.

'I've set us free.'

'Who are these humans?'

Roger didn't answer. They circled round, tails thrashing. Occasionally, one of them would hiss or snatch at the air with his claws. I took advantage of the break in the cat dialogue to introduce myself.

'You must be Wiggy,' I whispered.

'Yes,' he replied. 'I got here as quickly as I could.'

Suddenly, the Captain lashed out at Prideaux's throne, and broke one of its legs. Roger didn't flinch.

'It's over, Captain,' he said. 'Don't you feel it? We shouldn't fight. It's over.'

Astonishingly (and disarmingly), Roger dropped his fighting pose and sat opposite the Captain. It was a very deliberate action – showing extraordinary intellectual control – and the Captain watched him closely in some confusion. Roger pulled his body tight beneath him, and rested his weight very lightly on his delicate front paws. I noticed that his bloodied claws were now thoroughly retracted.

'What's happening?' I said to Wiggy.

'It looks like he's going to start telling a story.'

And so he was, in a way.

'For years and years,' Roger said, addressing us,

'all I've wanted is to tell my story. I told the first bit to you, didn't I, Wiggy?' he said.

'That's right,' said Wiggy. 'We got to about 1945.'

'I told the first bit to Jo, too. Also to Michael the potter, and to six other people. Every single time, Prideaux prevented me from telling it all. So I have never told the rest of my story to a living soul, and now——?' He laughed, effectively. 'Now, I never shall. The things that happened here. The way the Captain suffered here under Seeward. The unspeakable things Seeward made the Captain do — to *kittens*.'

Wiggy gasped and looked at me. I pulled a face to indicate I'd heard about the kittens already, but that I still thought it was shocking. We both looked at the Captain for his reaction. He relaxed his fighting position. He was listening.

'Seeward was a monster,' Roger continued. 'But cats trusted him. The Captain trusted him, didn't you, dear Captain, with your simple nature?'

The black cat closed his eyes and hung his head.

'He used you,' Roger added.

A tear trickled down the Captain's face.

'And he made you commit the ultimate betrayal. I know you resisted him; I know you tried. But in the end you let him try to ruin *me* — your own dear Roger! A cat you had created; a cat you had wept for; a cat you had roamed all of war-torn Europe looking for after you got separated from him in Athens.'

Poor Captain! Despite his record of casual homicide, I had often imagined his despair when he got back to the Acropolis from Piraeus to find no trace of Roger — just those skinny Greek cats (those bastards) rejoicing and jeering at his companion's humiliating capture.

'Tell them where you looked for me,' Roger said.

'Italy,' said the Captain. 'Then France, Germany, Poland.' He tailed off.

Roger prompted him again. 'How long did you look for me abroad?'

'Six years,' said the Captain.

We all made tut-tutting noises of sympathy.

'And he was only in the British Museum!' exclaimed Wiggy.

All eyes were turned to the Captain, who appeared lost in sadness and remorse.

'Wiggy, did you happen to bring that little thing you found at the library?' Roger said, lightly.

'Ooh, yes.'

I was puzzled. What thing?

The Captain was puzzled too — and a bit suspicious. 'Roger?' he said.

But Roger shrugged it off, as if to say that the little thing from the library was nothing at all to worry about.

'When I told the story of my Acropolis abduction to Wiggy,' Roger went on, still addressing the Captain, 'I described how you had gone off to Piraeus to find out about the boats to Brindisi.'

'I had. I went on the bus.'

'And do you remember, Wiggy, that I talked about the Captain's last words to me when he left me that morning?'

Wiggy hesitated. 'I'm not sure,' he said.

The Captain broke in. 'I said, "Roger, I'll always look after you."'

I felt quite choked up. In fact, we all did. Roger, the Captain, Wiggy and myself — everyone started sniffing. The only one of us quite unmoved was Watson, who — I'm embarrassed to say this — had happily gone to sleep.

Roger approached the Captain and put his paws on the big cat's shoulders.

'You gave me everything, Captain,' he said,

steadily. 'You showed me what a cat could be! Our ancestors were like you and me. They were strong and clever, and if someone had told them that cats of the future would be so feeble, they would have wept. We are the last of the Great Cats, Captain. But the price we paid for our immortality was subjection to the Cat Master – and now he's gone.'

'Isn't there another Cat Master to take over?' I asked. (It had been worrying me.)

'No. Prideaux was too arrogant to name one.'

The Captain sighed. 'Do you remember when we were on a boat once, at night, in the Aegean?'

Roger nodded.

'It was the happiest moment of my life,' the Captain said. And then he started to recite the lines from Tennyson's 'Ulysses' ('*That which we are, we are*'), which I needn't dwell on because everyone in the world knows them quite well by now because of Judi Dench doing them in *Skyfall*.

Over the Captain's shoulder, Roger made a signal with his head to Wiggy, and Wiggy withdrew something from his pocket. It looked like a cat collar.

Roger nodded. Wiggy reached down and stealthily put it round the Captain's neck. Lost in emotion (and Victorian poetry), the Captain hardly noticed what was happening.

Roger withdrew his paws from the Captain's shoulders. 'Shall we go outside?' he said.

Watson woke up when I opened the door. He trotted along to join me, and we all went outside in the snow – Roger leading the way, with the Captain – dazed and subdued – behind him, then Wiggy, Watson and me in a line.

'What's with the collar?' I whispered to Wiggy.

'It's the Great Debaser,' Wiggy explained, evidently surprised that I didn't know.

'Where did you get it?'

'You saw it in that card drawer in the library, Alec; but you didn't know what it was. I went and got it! I wrote to you about it this morning – but of course you didn't get the email.'

I was impressed. Wiggy had really come up trumps. Meanwhile Roger's plan had gone extremely well. He had now deprived the Captain of both his powers and his immortality. It seemed to me, in fact, that the work had been done, and we should perhaps break it up now, head for the nearest conurbation, get warm, have a big dinner, and either all go our separate ways, or maybe Roger would come and live with Watson and me, and finally get the rest of his story off his chest. As we crunched our way through the fresh snow in the wintry orchard, I did a new calculation.

Alec 0   Cats I

It looked as if this would be the final score.

By now we had reached the famous well – the one I'd seen Seeward posing beside, with the Captain sitting in the bucket. Roger jumped up on the stone wall; the Captain jumped up beside him.

'I feel really bad,' said the Captain. 'I'm so sorry about everything, Roger.'

He then looked at me and Wiggy. 'Was it your wife I met in that garden in Cambridge?' he asked me.

I was seriously taken aback.

'I was only looking for Winterton,' he said. 'I didn't hurt her. I just gave her a shock, I think. She fell down and then she didn't move.'

I felt furious. 'What do you mean, you gave her a shock?' I snapped. '*How* did you give her a shock?'

'Well, I'm not sure exactly,' he said, still sounding

quite apologetic. 'But probably by saying, "Hello, I'm looking for Winterton."'

Roger decided to retake control of proceedings.

'I have a few last words to say to you all,' he said. He looked so beautiful in the moonlight; in a magnificent manner, he addressed us each in turn. 'Alec, Hamlet is right. A man's life really is no more than to say *one*. Wiggy, give up on the screenplays.' Then he turned to Watson. 'Education never ends, Watson. It is a series of lessons with the greatest for the last.'

And with that he placed his paws either side of the Captain's neck once more. Then, with the barest effort, he bent them both sideways over the well, and they both fell in. If I live to be a hundred, it's a sight I will never forget.

'Roger, no!' I cried.

'Roger, no!' yelled the Captain as well, arguably with even more reason.

We rushed to the well, and Watson jumped up but I caught him — thank God I caught him before he fell in after them — but I also caught the fleeting sight of the two cats falling, together, locked in each other's limbs, the Captain's eyes huge with fright.

Wiggy and I stood there, too shocked to move. Roger had gone. With a magnificent final Watson address from Sherlock Holmes, he had taken the Reichenbach Falls way out, and the final score was, after all, 2–1 in favour of Alec.

So that's nearly the end, and I'd like to finish my account with an apology. Reading it all back, I realise that at times I have been a tad flippant in the way I have written this, and I have also told the story with what appears to be a lamentable lack of narrative organisation. To these quite reasonable objections, I shall return (when I've decided what to say).

I am back at home in Cambridge now, and the adorable Watson is safely at my feet. We are both recovering from our respective ordeals, but I often wake up sweating, remembering how I caught his little body as he tried to jump after those evil cats into that fateful well. I wish I could say that spring is round the corner, but it isn't. It is still absolutely freezing, and the weather forecasters have run out of jocular ways of breaking the miserable news that this state of affairs will continue for the next two months at least. Speaking of the weather,

Wiggy and I were snowbound in Dorset for three days after the events at Harville, and I think we helped each other through it. He's a chap with hidden depths, despite the predicted floppy hair and mustard-coloured trousers. It was amazing that he understood from Seeward's pamphlet what the Great Debaser was, and even more amazing that he remembered my description of a bit of leather with a buckle in the Seeward card-catalogue drawer in Prideaux's office.

Having reached the end, I feel I must now revise my answers to the quiz I set myself earlier.

I. Did things turn out well, generally speaking, Alec?
Yes, very well ☐   No ☑   Not really ☐   Don't ask ☐

I think you will agree this is much nearer the mark than 'Not really'.

2. If NO, was it your own fault? (Think carefully)
Yes, I feel terrible ☐   No ☑   Not really ☐   Don't ask ☐

Yes, I have come to terms with my own lack of responsibility, at last. My only sin, in retrospect, was to be so obsessed with this story.

3. Was anyone hurt?

Yes ☑   No ☐   Not really ☐   Don't ask ☐

I feel sorry for the cats, especially Roger. But I have no sympathy at all for Julian Prideaux. After all that eyeball-flashing, I quite enjoyed seeing his blood flying about like that. It seemed like his due comeuppance for a) being an Evil Cat Master in league with Beelzebub, doling out death to innocent humans just in order to punish the wilful Roger, and also b) all those bloody departmental meetings he didn't turn up to. I had no idea my professional resentment went so deep.

4. Has the world been rid of the evil cats?

Miraculously, yes ☐   Worryingly, no ☐   Too early to tell ☑

Wishful thinking, this. It's just that I have dreams of Roger somehow climbing out of that well and coming to live with us. After all, unlike the Captain, he was not wearing the Great Debaser and therefore retained his powers, perhaps. What a team we would make: me, the loyal Watson and a brilliant talking cat.

5. How do you feel about cats now?

Love them ☐   Indifferent ☐   Conflicted ☑   Hate them ☐

Yes, no change there.

6. How do you feel, facing the future?

Happy ☐   Relieved ☑   Numb ☐   Don't ask ☐

Not so numb, now that I've written my account.

7. Would you consider a holiday in Dorset in the near future?

Yes ☐   No ☐   Not on your life ☑

No change there either, I'm afraid.

I no longer care much about the gaps in this story, so I hope you don't either. I think I've made it clear that I asked *everybody* for enlightenment on even some of the niggling smaller details; I truly did my best. As you will have guessed, I did invent one small section of the narrative — Roger's telepathic 'e-miaow' exchange with Prideaux — but I feel it is authentically what must have happened, and I thoroughly enjoyed writing it, so there you are.

I did finally see the clip on YouTube that Wiggy

kept forgetting to send the link for. I now watch it over and over again. It's in colour, with sound, and it's a rerun of the rabbit experiment. It was filmed in 1964, just before Seeward killed himself. He uses the same curtain and a similar rabbit, but the cat this time is Roger. Seeward speaks to the camera – a thin, nasty voice; he pulls the curtain and Roger leaps up on to the table opposite the hapless bunny. But he doesn't kill it. He sits beautifully, serenely, while Seeward orders him to do it. He lifts a paw and examines its underside, before putting it down again. Such nonchalance. He even reaches out and gives the rabbit's flank a little pat. Seeward is evidently incensed, and the film ends. It's my conclusion – and there is now no one left alive from whom I can get any collaboration, so I'm on my own with it – that Roger's bold (and moral) refusenik attitude was the thing that broke Seeward's cat-master spirit and caused his suicide. The photograph of the two cats in the grass is not about hedonistic animals callously lazing in the shadow of a corpse (as it seemed on first sight); it's a moment of great emotional importance to Roger, as he comforts the enslaved Captain whom he will shortly leave behind, to become a cat fugitive for ever.

It has become clear to me that until he killed Prideaux on that night in Dorset, Roger had never killed anybody. The eight previous lives – including Jo's – were all taken by Prideaux, either to prevent Roger from telling the terrible secrets of Harville, or to remind him who was boss.

Having said I must apologise, I've turned quite unapologetic. I suppose that's because there *is* a good reason for the rather irresponsible way I've told this story – sometimes a bit flippantly, and letting my style degenerate unforgivably *with so many italics*, and allowing events to unfold just the way they did for me living through them, rather than organising the story properly, beginning at the beginning once I was in possession of all the facts. The thing is, my dear wife Mary loved to read mysteries – hence the name Watson for our stalwart little dog. I think I have mentioned how much I miss her. Well. There's no change there, either. This has been written for Mary, with all my love. I'm sure it's not good enough! But if I had written it in the conventional way, she would have guessed everything from about page six, because that's what she always did. This is not to say, however, that she wouldn't still have been two steps ahead of me, even with the story as it stands. She would have looked up from the manuscript, removed her old reading glasses, and said to me, reprovingly, 'Oh, *Bear.*'

A NOTE FROM THE
AUTHOR

About twenty years ago, some bookseller friends gave me a gift of a small wooden box with a tiny handmade book inside. The box was modern; the book had been made in 1934. It was handwritten, and the pages had been sewn together with strong cotton twine. On the front page were the words, *The Adaptable Cat. 2nd edition. Feb: 1934. By A.M.B.T.* Inside it said, *COPYRIGHT ORIGINAL* and, *Printed by the author A.M.B.T.* The dedication was: *To my friend Gatley I dedicate this little book. The genuine doings of my adaptable cat.* The book contained a poem about the cat (whose name was 'Huffy') and also seventeen black and white photographs that had been carefully tipped in. And what they showed was a handsome substantial tabby-and-white cat who lived a seemingly glorious and innocent life in a 1930s sunny garden, posing in wicker baskets and dollie outfits, and so on. Obviously I had no idea who 'A.M.B.T.' was, except that he once had a friend called Gatley. But his affection for his cat — and his appreciation for its adaptability (a quite unusual quality in cats, after all) — made a big impression on me.

I lost track of this little book quite a while ago. It turned up when I was moving house, just a few months after I'd finished writing *Cat Out Of Hell*, and I was thrilled to see it again. It's only after finishing a novel that you can sit back and think (sometimes with alarm), 'Well, where did all *that* come from?' Some of the influences on *Cat Out Of Hell* were direct enough: I have long been a fan of M.R. James, for example. I have pastiched him before, and I hope I shall do so again. I placed M.R. James's *Ghost Stories of an Antiquary* on the desk alongside Desmond Morris's *Catwatching*, Anne Rice's *Interview with the Vampire*, and also Patricia Highsmith's horrible *Animal Lover's Book of Beastly Murder* (which was much too dark for me). Thinking about horror in general, I consciously focused on recalling a book from my teenage years: a particular schlocky paperback collection of horror stories that always scared me, but attracted me as well. I could remember how it smelled, but what was it called? Finally, I remembered enough to track it down and re-buy it (*Great Stories of Mystery and Imagination*, edited by Bryan Douglas) – and I still shiver when I look at the clichéd cover: a ghoulish and cobwebby clergyman with blackened eye sockets, his bony fingers splayed on the top of a dusty dark-wood table (or is it a coffin?).

So there were some influences that were obvious. The 'Adaptable Cat' got into my narrative because of the photographs – even without being able to refresh my memory, I could draw on the intense way an old photograph of a long-ago cat could engage one's curiosity. Meanwhile *Catwatching* was a really rich source of ideas, because it asked questions such as 'Why do cats purr?' which I thought I could perhaps answer (fictionally) in new and convincing ways. 'Why do cats knead your lap before settling down?' Morris had asked, for example, and then explained that when a cat performs the motion on us, it is thinking of its kittenhood, when it needed to stimulate milk from the mother. Such an explanation was a revelation at the end of the 1980s, but I like to think we've moved on a bit now. Oh, how little they know of zoology, who only zoology know.

To be honest, the evil cat was top of my list when I was asked to write a horror novella. I had done evil cats before, and I'd loved it. Jeanette Winterson had asked me to contribute to a book of stories inspired by operas, and initially I expended quite a lot of effort just coming up with excuses, but finally I said that if I could think of a funny twist on the story of *The Turn of the Screw*, I'd do one. Of course, Benjamin Britten's *The Turn of the Screw* is based on the Henry James story in which an imaginative governess grows convinced that the two children in her care (Miles and Flora) are possessed by evil spirits. At the heart of the story, it's ambiguous: is she right about what is happening, or is she mad? However, having volunteered *The Turn of the Screw*, I then couldn't think of any sort of comic twist, and so I just started making excuses again.

But then I was saved. At the time, I was the owner of two brother-and-sister rescue cats — Bill and Daisy – who were a very depressing presence in my life. Basically, they rejected my love, scratched my face off if they got the chance, and were incapable of joy. They also made no noise whatsoever, which was very disconcerting. Customarily, they sat at the top of the stairs, together, in silence – two black, forbidding shapes, Bill quite big, and Daisy quite little. (I have a photograph of them assuming this terrifying silhouette, which makes people fall about laughing.) Anyway, one day I was climbing the stairs, approaching them, and I broke down. 'Why won't you let me love you?' I wailed. And then, like a switch being thrown, I saw that I resembled the governess in *The Turn of the Screw*! I wrote the story from the point of view of a male friend of a woman with a history of letting her imagination run away with her. Disregarding his advice, she daringly gives the names Miles and Flora to some horrible brother-and-sister rescue cats. It proves to be a fatal mistake.

As for Roger being a talking cat, well, the idea seems quite commonplace to me. Of course, sometimes cat-owners do feel their cats *are* talking to them. A friend of mine says to his cat each evening, 'Do you want dinner later, or do you want it now?' And the cat says, '*Niaow.*' But in fictional terms, well, there must have been scary old Czechoslovakian folk tales that I read as a child, and then there was also *Top Cat* on the TV, where the cat was a Manhattanite lord of misrule (in a jaunty necktie) and talked like Phil Silvers. People have asserted that the main influence on my *Cat Out Of Hell* is self-evidently Mikhail Bulgakov's *The Master and Margarita*, but since I've never read it, it can't be. Much nearer to the mark would be the short story 'Tobermory' by Saki (H.H. Munro). In this classic story, the cat at a country house is given the power of speech – and everyone is thrilled when he speaks his first words (on being offered milk), 'I don't mind if I do.' But then it starts to go wrong.

Tobermory fixed his gaze serenely on the middle distance. It was obvious that boring questions lay outside his scheme of life.

'What do you think of human intelligence?' asked Mavis Pellington lamely.

'Of whose intelligence in particular?' asked Tobermory, coldly.

'*Oh, well, mine for instance,*' said Mavis, with a feeble laugh.

'*You put me in an embarrassing position,*' said Tobermory.

'*When your inclusion in this house-party was suggested, Sir Wilfrid protested that you were the most brainless woman of his acquaintance, and that there was a wide distinction between hospitality and the care of the feeble-minded. Lady Blemley replied that your lack of brain-power was the precise quality which had earned you your invitation, as you were the only person she could think of who might be idiotic enough to buy their old car. You know, the one they call 'The Envy of Sisyphus', because it goes quite nicely up-hill if you push it.*'

So what a mish-mash of influences. The structure of the book comes from memories of the great Gothic novels such as Mary Shelley's *Frankenstein* – and there are conscious allusions to other historical narratives of the nineteenth century. But it's fascinating, after the event, to pinpoint stuff that you didn't know was in your mind at all. One of the darker inspirations for a key scene in the book, I now realise, was an installation I saw a few years back at the Hayward Gallery – and at the time I certainly didn't think, 'One day I will use this in a book.' Nor did I remember it until I was writing the scene, when all I could remember about it was the feeling it inculcated of icy apprehension. It turns out it was called 'In Memory of H.P. Lovecraft', and it was by Mike Nelson. A bleak space (of two rooms) painted plain white, it had been rendered utterly terrifying by wild gashes and claw-marks on the bottom half of the walls.

Of all these influences, I like to think it was *Top Cat* that made the biggest contribution in the end. My cat Roger is certainly effectual and intellectual. His story is drawn from zoological speculations, artistic installations, and also those inseparable James brothers, M.R. and Henry. But one really never knows what's been stored away in one's head. When I was finally reunited with *The Adaptable Cat*, I opened it and reread it. And yes, it is a sunny tale of a sunny garden between the wars. The cat looks like Roger, being tabby and white. He poses in his dollie costume, and he sits in that basket. But there is more. He poses with a rabbit! (I had completely forgotten this when I wrote the rabbit scene of John Seeward's cine film). And then it turns out he has a friend – and what is it? A dog, maybe? A kitten? No, it is an enormous black cat, who in the photograph genuinely seems to have more the proportions of a bear. I look at this huge black cat, standing on his hind legs with his front paws on the edge of a goldfish bowl that has been placed on a stool in the garden. Roger is looking at the goldfish, too. I look at them — those long-deceased cats from 1934, beloved photographic subjects of the mysterious 'A.M.B.T.' — I look at them over and over. Because there is no doubt in my mind. It is Roger, and it is the Captain! All this time I had actual photographs of Roger and the Captain, and I didn't even know.

Lynne Truss
July 2014

ALSO AVAILABLE FROM HAMMER

Touched

Joanna Briscoe

Rowena Crale and her family have moved from London.

They now live in a small English village in a cottage which seems to be resisting all attempts at renovation.

Walls ooze damp, stains come through layers of wallpaper, celings sag.

And strange noises – voices – emanate from empty rooms.

As Rowena struggles with the upheaval of builders while trying to be a dutiful wife and a good mother to her young children, her life starts to disintegrate.

And then, one by one, her daughters go missing . . .

ALSO AVAILABLE FROM HAMMER

Breakfast with the Borgias
DBC Pierre

'Hell is other people.' A chilling, page-turning Hammer novella by **DBC Pierre, the Booker-Prize-winning author of *Vernon God Little*.**

The setting: a faded, lonely guesthouse on the Suffolk coast. Outside, it's dark and very foggy. Inside, there's no phone or internet reception, no hope of connectivity with the outside world.

Enter Ariel Panek, a promising young academic en route from the USA to a convention in Amsterdam. With his plane grounded at Stansted, he has been booked in for the night at the guesthouse.

Discombobulated and jetlagged, he falls in with a family who appear to be commemorating an event.

But this is no ordinary commemoration. And this is no ordinary family.

As evening becomes night, Panek realises that he has become caught in an insidious web of other people's secrets and lies, a Sartrian hell from which there may be for him no escape . . .

'A thoroughly modern nightmare . . . DBC Pierre stacks up the layers of horror with relish and skill'
The Times

HAMMER
AN EXCLUSIVE MEDIA COMPANY

ALSO AVAILABLE FROM HAMMER

The Woman in Black:
Angel of Death
Martyn Waites

**The fully authorised chilling sequel to Susan Hill's bestselling
ghost-story, *The Woman in Black*.**

1940: World War Two

A group of school children and their teacher escape the London
Blitz and arrive at a lonely, desolate house – where someone is
waiting for them.

She is someone the children cannot see, but she is far more
dangerous and deadly than the German bombs.
She is ...

The Woman in Black

**SOON TO BE A MAJOR FILM STARRING
JEREMY IRVINE AND PHOEBE FOX**

About Hammer

Hammer is the most well-known film brand in the UK, having made over 150 feature films which have been terrifying and thrilling audiences worldwide for generations.

Whilst synonymous with horror and the genre-defining classics it produced in the 1950s to 1970s, Hammer was recently rebooted in the film world as the home of "Smart Horror", with the critically acclaimed *Let Me In* and *The Woman in Black*. With *The Woman in Black: Angel of Death* scheduled for 2015, Hammer has been re-born.

Hammer's literary legacy is also now being revived through its new partnership with Arrow Books. This series features original novellas by some of today's most celebrated authors, as well as classic stories from nearly a century of production.

In 2014 Hammer Arrow has published books by DBC Pierre, Lynne Truss and Joanna Briscoe as well as a novelisation of the forthcoming *The Woman in Black: Angel of Death*, continuing a programme that began with bestselling novellas from Helen Dunmore and Jeanette Winterson. Beautifully produced and written to read in a single sitting, Hammer Arrow books are perfect for readers of quality contemporary fiction.

For more information on Hammer
visit: www.hammerfilms.com or
www.facebook.com/hammerfilms